THE CARIBBEAN CHRONICLES

DOWN TO DAVY JONES

EDDIE JONES

DRY BONES PUBLISHING

A Stormy Voyage: Battling Demonic Fury and Leaky Vessels

From a blackened sky, the storm screamed with demonic fury. Rain pelted the vessel's deck above us, driving our haggard crew below. With each wobbling claw up the back of a wave, the leaky ship creaked and groaned in long, agonizing moans.

Oops, sorry. I meant to say that with each wobbling tug on the oars, the backs of the crew creaked, and men groaned in long agonizing moans.

The ship also made sounds, mostly of a sloshing, sinking sort.

I sat hunched forward on a wooden bench similar to the type you might find in a primitive church crowded with men, none of whom smelled as if they were fond of bathing. I was in the center of the middle pew grasping the end of a long oar that fed out through an open port. I promise I am not going to whine about how I ended up experiencing another epileptic absence seizure.

Instead, I chose to project a positive outlook like the great explorer Marco Polo, who traveled along the Silk Road from Europe to Asia between 1271 and 1295—waving to peasants who wielded pitchforks and called, "Marco! Polo!" before ducking behind stone walls and snickering to one another. "That Marco Polo, what an oaf. Only an idiot wears a fox-fur shawl, puffy pants, and bedroom slippers to go swimming."

But this was a different time and that time was the Age of Exploration and swimsuits had not yet been invented. So after blindly flailing around in water up to his chest while trying to locate giggling boys and girls dressed in nothing more than undergarments, Marco would emerge—soaked, skin shriveled like an old man, hairs matted on his fox-fur shawl—and open his eyes. Only then would the son of Mr. Polo realize that he stood in the water alone. With his white pantaloon pants ruined from water tainted with urine, this champion of exploration would think to himself, *I bet if I had a logo on my shirt with a guy riding a horse and carrying a big stick, the other kids in Latin class would not make fun of me.*

Such was the positive outlook Marco Polo emitted. Also, due to the fact that scented soap and deodorant had not yet been invented, Marco Polo also emitted a stench very much like that of the men seated around me.

"Bend your backs, ladies," barked the quartermaster, "or you'll have no backs to bend!" *Snap! Snap!*

The ship's quartermaster barked lots of orders. His was a loud and snarling breed of barkers. Bare-chested, with arms the thickness of a main spar and wearing what appeared to be a cloth adult diaper kept in place by a leather belt, the quartermaster struck an imposing figure with his bullwhip. In this case, the imposing figure was a rather largish man hunched over his oar.

Snap! Snap! Upon receiving the lash, the hunched man tumbled face-first onto the floor.

"Ah, sir," said the imposing figure's neighbor, "I think Kamaul is dead."

Snap! "No dying while rowing." *Snap! Snap!* "And no jawing about dying while rowing, do I make myself clear?"

"AYE, SIR!"

A figure appeared in the doorway. "Sir, the Squire demands your presence."

"Tell him I'm busy trying to whip these men into shape," replied Barking Bart.

"He thought you might say that and warned that if you did not come at once he would order you to give yourself the lash."

Barking Bart coiled his whip and hooked it in a loop on his adult diaper's belt. "Bend your backs into it, ladies, or—"

"We 'ill 'ave no backs to bend, sir!" the men said in unison.

No sooner had Barking Bart started toward the exit when he wheeled and glared at me. "I'm keeping my eye on you, Little Shrimp."

With that less-than-encouraging warning, the ship's quartermaster left the rowing deck, and the crew breathed a sigh of relief. Then, due to the crew's bad breath, the crew gagged.

To those around me, my neighbor whispered, "I fear a man will soon be sacrificed to appease the gods."

I said nothing. Being new to the ship, and from all appearances the youngest, I did not wish to stand out or inhale.

"And not just any man," said my other neighbor. "But the one who invited this hellish squall that has descended upon us."

Not an expert on meteorology or ocean weather patterns or the whims of weather gods, I kept my head down. Also, I was pretty sure my neighbor meant me.

"Should this continue," the man behind me said, "this vessel will go down within hours."

"Perhaps minutes."

"We should toss the lad now," my neighbor said.

"Yes, toss the Little Shrimp," said my neighbor in front. Due to the fact that my neighbor in front lacked most of his teeth, what he actually said was, "Toss the Whittle Shrimp."

"Toss Whittle Shrimp." The men around me snickered, then chanted, "Toss the Whittle Shrimp. Toss the Whittle Shrimp."

With the mob's chant growing louder, Barking Bart returned with a well-dressed man. Well-dressed in the sense that he had on trousers, shirt, vest, coat, and shoes. By comparison, the men in the crew were down to threadbare loincloths.

"Ladies, this be the Squire," said Barking Bart. "He owns the cargo on this tub and wishes to see it delivered on time."

The fancily dressed man looked us over, walking back and forth with his hands clasped behind his back, a scowl of disapproval on his portly face. "How goes the rowing?"

"The men seem to lack incentive," answered Barking Bart.

Stroking his white, pointy beard, the Squire asked, "Have you given them the lash?"

"Aye, and often."

"And rats? Have you unleashed the rats?"

"I have, but after nibbling a toe or two, the vermin scamper away. It's the odor, sir. Even rats have standards, low though they may be."

Tugging so hard that he pulled hairs from his white, pointy beard, the Squire said, "Then put the fear of death in the men. Select a man for keel hauling."

The crew gasped. Then they coughed due to the stench they inhaled.

"Are you sure?" Barking Bart asked. "Losing even one man to keel hauling will cut into our speed."

"If it is motivation the men need, it is motivation they will receive," replied the Squire.

"Not keel hauling," whispered my neighbor. "Anything but keel hauling."

A young man sprouting sparse whiskers on his chin and lip asked, "Is keel hauling bad?"

"Why, there be nothin' worse," replied my neighbor. "First, the victim is tied to one end of a long rope. Then he's thrown overboard and dragged under the ship's keel, sinking back along the length of her hull until he crashes inter the rudder. If at that point the poor chap be not drowned, he's pulled aboard, hauled ter the bow, and dropped over again so as ter repeat the process."

"Even if the victim survives the first dunkin'," another man piped up, "the second dunkin' 'ill usually finish him off."

"You!" Barking Bart pointed at me. "On your feet."

"Me?" I asked.

Barking Bart snapped his whip over my head in a threatening manner. "Rest of you scalawags back into it, or—"

"We 'ill 'ave no backs to bend, sir!"

"Might make a decent crew yet," mumbled Barking Bart. "You, Little Shrimp, with me. A dip and trip under the ship will make quick work of you."

"Toss Whittle Shrimp!" the men chanted. "Toss Whittle Shrimp! Toss Whittle Shrimp!"

Barking Bart gave me a wry smile. "Not popular with the crew?"

"Guess not," I replied.

"We'll see if you're more popular with sharks ... *Whittle Shrimp*."

CHAPTER ONE

A STORM OF ACCUSATIONS AND FATEFUL CHOICES

On-deck sails billowed red in the glow of a ship's lantern. Waves smashed into the bow, showering the men with frigid water. The wind tore through the rigging with the force of a thousand strong hands threatening to shred the sails.

"Men, it be time for keelhaul practice!"

At Barking Bart's command, sailors climbed down from the rigging like spiders. Judging from the looks of relief on their faces, most preferred keelhauling practice to dangling from flimsy pieces of wood and netting while hurricane-force winds ripped away their loincloths. I could not see how dragging me in the water alongside the ship would accomplish much. I mean, sure, I'd drown, but there were faster ways to dispose of me. Throwing me overboard, for one. But then I'm no great ocean-crossing sailor. Not like Vasco da Gama or even Christopher Columbus, who, even when he landed on a completely different continent insisting he had reached India, practiced what's called the "illusory truth effect." Basically, it's a phenomenon whereby people believe a lie if it is read, heard, and repeated enough. Today, we call this the internet.

My point is, dragging a body alongside an already slow and lumbering vessel would only cause the leaky tub to go slower. Barking Bart should have known this … and did.

"Perhaps it be best to simply have you jump overboard and be done with it. Keelhauling might slow us down."

"Or not and simply say I did," I replied. "I'm happy to hide until the storm passes. The rest of the crew never has to know."

"The rest of the crew never has to know what?" a voice asked from behind us.

Over my shoulder, through stinging rain, I spotted a short, round man approaching.

"What does the crew never need to know?" the round man again asked Barking Bart.

"The lad and me were discussing keelhauling, Captain. It was the Squire's idea," Barking Bart explained. "He believes the men need incentive."

"And you?" the ship's pilot asked.

"I believe in the rod and whip and a fist to the lip. Less spoilage. Plus, it gives me a chance to flex my muscles."

"The Squire does not command this vessel, nor does he give orders," said the pilot. "We need every able-bodied man, small and large, to pull their weight."

"Aye, but as you can see, the weight of this shrimp be near nothing."

Turning to the crew gathered around us, the pilot shouted over shrieking wind and bashing waves, "All hands below! Assemble in the cargo hold!"

Grumbling about missing out on watching one of the crew drown as punishment, men descended into the hatch.

"That means you," he said to Barking Bart. "And the lad as well."

While we fell in behind the crew and pilot, Barking Bart whispered to me, "I not be done with this keelhauling business, Whittle Shrimp. Not by a long shot."

In the bowels of the ship, I stood in ankle-deep water that reeked of urine and other body fluids. Before us, the ship's pilot held a clay-pot lantern, offering only enough light to illuminate the worried faces of crew and cargo—in this case slaves.

"Judging by the weather, the gods have it in for us," the pilot said. "I fear we will not last the night."

"She's a strong ship," the Squire said. "Had her built with the best timbers from Tyre. We only need the men to row harder."

"Have you seen the sails?" asked the ship's pilot. "They're little more than tassels. Neptune himself could not sail us out of this squall."

"And yet you, sir, are charged with doing just that," the Squire said to the pilot.

Shifting blame, the pilot announced, "One of you is responsible for bringing this disaster upon us, and I mean to find out which of you it is. Perhaps if we rid this vessel of that infidel, it will please the gods."

"That be what I was trying to do with the keelhauling," said Barking Bart. "Get rid of entrails."

One of the crew whispered to Barking Bart, "infidel not entrails."

"I say entrails." Making his point with a fat fist, Barking Bart boxed the ear of the crewmember. "What say you now?"

"Entrails," the man mumbled.

"No need to ask the gods," said my rowing neighbor. "It's the lad's fault, I'm sure of it."

"Lad's fault! Lad's fault!" the crew chanted.

"I say we slide a dirk in Whittle Shrimp's ribs," the man behind me said. "See if that pleases the gods."

Holding his lantern high, the pilot interrogated a smallish man seated alone on a sack of soggy grain. "Except for this lad we fetched from the sea, all are slaves or hired crew. "But you," the pilot to the man on the sack, "you booked passage on this vessel as a passenger. Our only passenger. Where do you come from? What god do you worship?"

Straightening himself, the small man answered, "I am Jonah, son of Amittai, a Hebrew. I worship the god Yahweh who made the heavens, seas, and dry land."

At this revelation, the men gasped.

The pilot asked, "What have you done to offend this god you serve?"

"Tell us plain, man," the Squire demanded. "Is your god angry with you? Is that the reason my cargo and ship are in peril?"

"Due to the grievous evil committed by the people of Nineveh, to that great city commanded by God I go," the Hebrew answered. "'Against it, you are to preach,' said my God. But refused did I. To Joppa, I fled. Boarded this vessel there did I."

"And you," the ship's pilot said to me. "Since we hauled you aboard in the black of night, we have endured nothing but wind and rain and waves. Are you also cursed by this god?"

I gulped, unsure how, or if, I should answer—the concept of baptism being one of those activities that even in religious circles can be difficult to explain.

"Leave the lad alone," said the Hebrew, "for it is I alone who has offended Yahweh."

"And you?" the pilot said to me. "How did you end up in the sea?"

With all the crew watching, I said, "My mother is, ah, sick, so I, ah ... went down to the docks and, ah ..."

"Out with it," said Barking Bart.

"Went into a creek to be baptized, but when the preacher pushed me under—"

From overhead, a loud *BOOM* shook the leaky vessel.

"The mast is gone!" shouted the pilot.

"The mast is gone!" yelled the crew.

The Squire asked, "The mast is gone?"

"Hebrew must go!" the men shouted. "Hebrew must go!"

"I blame you, Shrimp," growled Barking Bart.

"I will not have an innocent man's blood on my hands," said the pilot. "Cast lots. We will let the gods decide."

With his gaze fixed on me, Barking Bart sliced his palm with a dagger and smeared one stick among many with blood. One by one the men reached into the pouch to see if the lot fell to them. All picked a bloodless stick.

When at last the pouch reached the Hebrew, he said to me, "Sent onto this vessel for a purpose are you." He thrust his hand into the pouch. "To a great adventure called are you." Withdrawing his fist, the Hebrew clutched his stick, passing me the bag with his free hand.

"Only thing I know I'm called to do is graduate high school with honors so I can get into a decent college. Honestly, though, I'd just like to have more time to travel."

"Fear you must the hounds of hell who bark loudest," the Hebrew continued.

I couldn't tell if he meant Barking Bart, but already I'd decided I didn't like the way he bullied the crew and me. With fingers fumbling, I reached inside and felt wood and sticky wetness.

"Die for all one man should," said the Hebrew, "than perish every soul aboard."

With a half-smile, the Hebrew uncoiled his fingers. A narrow smear of blood streaked one side of his stick. Before I could open my fist, the men rushed the Hebrew, pulling him toward the ladder.

"This not be over, Shrimp," Barking Bart snarled at me. "Not by a long shot."

"Oh, but I think it is," I said, making a fist around my wet stick.

Topside, Jonah, son of Amittai, showed no fear.

"Here you go, you gods of the sea," Barking Bart yelled. "This be our sacrifice. Do with him as you wish."

"Gods be appeased!" cried the crew. "Gods be appeased!"

"Gods be a peas?" asked Barking Bart.

Jonah, son of Amittai, fell over the side into blackness.

The men erupted in cheers and jeers. Such was the heartless crew with which I sailed. But if they expected to appease the gods with their human sacrifice, they were greatly mistaken, for no sooner had their chant died down when, from behind the ship, an enormous wave approached. Only this was not your normal Waimea Bay big wave, but rather an enormous, blackish sea monster rising from the deep—one with a giant red eye and tentacles longer than the ship.

"Sink me!" the Squire screamed. "It's the Kraken!"

CHAPTER TWO

A Terrifying Encounter with a Giant Squid

"**A**rm yourselves, men! Kill that giant squid before it kills us!" Wheeling, Barking Bart glared at me. "That goes for you too, Shrimp."

To be honest, I have never believed there was a creature called the Kraken. I know authors who write fantasy novels will sometimes feature the Kraken in stories to show that sailing can be dangerous. And sailing *is* dangerous. For example, on average every year one hundred and fifty boats are lost at sea.

To put this into perspective, 160,000 smartphones are lost each day.

In the last decade, there were 271 deaths while boating. The number one cause of death was, you guessed it—the Kraken. Just kidding. The main cause of death at sea is drowning. Most weren't wearing life jackets. In only 28 percent of the cases were adverse weather conditions mentioned as the cause of death. My point is, if you're going offshore, you should probably put on a life jacket and worry less about the Kraken.

That's my main point.

I could go into great detail about how I frantically searched for a weapon to beat off the Kraken, but I'll get right to the bad of the story—at least bad from my perspective.

The Kraken grabbed Barking Bart and flung him overhead. That might sound like good news, but as he sailed overhead and into the sea, he yelled, "This be your fault, Shrimp! Mark my words, there will be hell to pay. Hound you to hell and back I—"

And then he was gone.

I sighed, tossed away the puny piece of rigging I'd picked up to beat away the Kraken, and started for a deck hatch.

Even though bodies lay strewn about a ship that was quickly sinking, I hadn't asked to be on the ship, so in that moment I still held out hope that I would suddenly snap out of my absence seizure and find myself back on shore next to Mom.

Then, with great speed, tentacles slithered across the deck, crushing railings, peeling up planks, and tearing down rigging. A feeler suddenly coiled around my ankles. Squeezing tight, sharp, horny suckers tore at my flesh. With a violent jerk, the sea monster pulled me off my feet and in a violent snapping motion, flung me into the raging sea.

CHAPTER THREE

BIBLE LESSONS AND SEA MONSTER MEALS

Jonah and the Whale ... true story or fiction? Where you come down on Jonah's "whale of a tale" probably depends on if and where and how frequently you attended church as a kid. It may also depend on if an enormous octopus swallowed you.

I learned a lot about boats and sailing and seafarers like Jonah, Noah, and Moses (short float in a tiny boat) in those few brief weeks in Vacation Bible School. I also learned that even moms who are not necessarily religious sometimes use VBS as a cheap babysitting service. Those three hours from six to nine at night were just enough time for my mom to grab drinks and dinner with her girlfriends.

The point is, my VBS teacher was always careful to make clear that no one knew for certain if it was a whale or some other fish that swallowed Jonah. She would all but shout, "THE BIBLE DOESN'T SAY IT WAS A WHALE."

Clearly, our VBS teacher did not want to get into a deep discussion of the feeding habits of the largest known mammal in the ocean, and for good reason. One of the really smart kids would mention how a human can't survive three days in the belly of a sea creature as large as the Antarctic blue whale—even though some can weigh up to 400,000 pounds. Do you know what else weighs 400,000 pounds? Thirty-three elephants. Antarctic blue whales have also been known to reach a hundred feet in length. That is as long as a 737 airplane. During its main feeding season, even just *one* of these behemoth aquatic mammals can eat around 7,936 pounds of krill per day.

Your average boy in school consumes zero pounds of krill in a day.

All of this was going through my mind as I settled into the Kraken's gastric gut. In pitch-black darkness, surrounded by flipping and flopping fish, I held my breath due to the vapors of decomposing krill.

You know how in a scary movie when a teen is trapped all by himself in a spooky house with all the lights off and the floor joists are making scary groaning noises and the kid is huddled by himself in a corner because he knows, looking back on it, he should have listened to his friends when they warned, *Do not sneak into the old Zuckerberg place. That creepy old man is watching your every move.* And right then someone wearing a Halloween mask made to look like Jeff Bezos appears next to the boy and whispers, "Boo!"

You know that scene? That's sort of what happened.

"You? In the fish belly?"

Startled to hear the Hebrew speak, I gasped. Then I felt nauseous due to vapors from decomposing krill.

"No man alive hath descended to the depths of the dead and returned, but rebelled against the great I Am, have I. For my offense, pay I must. But you, lad, to the depths of the sea, what offense led you?"

Not wishing to get into a lengthy discussion with the Hebrew about how my baptism in a creek had gone terribly wrong, I kept my mouth shut. Choosing not to inhale seemed like the smart move.

"Fear, you do, of losing your mother, but fear more, you must, the one who is able to destroy both soul and body."

Rumbling in the Kraken's tummy sent giant squid fart bubbles exploding in my face.

"Find the one who conquered the grave, you must. He alone can raise you from the dead."

Stuffed into a sticky, stinking Kraken gut, contracting muscles squeezed me. If you've ever watched the Space Shuttle launch from Kennedy Space Center, you know how explosive it is when all that volatile propellant erupts and the rocket ship hurls skyward. What you may not know is that sometimes in the test, simulator pilots black out due to G forces.

That's sort of what happened next. Forced upward through krill sludge, the gut of the Kraken shook violently and vomited me out.

CHAPTER FOUR

SEEKING SANCTUARY IN THE HAUNTED BELFRY

"Ex, ex, excuse ... *burrrp,* excuse ... *bwaaaah,* beg yer pardon."

Face down on hard-packed sand, the faint voice calling to me jarred me awake. A sweltering dampness pressed upon me. Pulling my feet clear of sizzling hot water washing over my ankles and calves, I studied the yellow-brown beach cloaked in a steamy mist.

"Mind, mind ... *bah,* mind scooting over? You're on top of my jug."

I rolled onto my back and looked up. A figure stood over me. Clothed in a long black frock and black trousers, his gray, wiry beard grew from his cheek and chin bones, extending all the way to the collar of his white blood-soaked shirt.

"Say, you look familiar. You ever ... *bah,* you ever been ter ... *burrrp,* you ever sailed ter Port Royal?"

No skin on bones. No lips or eyes. Only a skull with a black patch covering one eye socket.

"Don't think so."

"Me neither. Must 'ave been a couple other fellers."

Bending down, he snagged the jug's curved handle with a hook protruding from the end of his frock's sleeve. "What brings you ter ... *bwaaaah,* what brings you ter ... *bah.*" He took a long gulp from the jug, spilling golden liquid down the front of his shirt. "How'd you end up on this beach?"

For as far as I could see, bones and rotting bodies lay piled in great heaps. "A baptism gone bad."

"Aye, trick ... trick ... *burrrp*, tricky business a getting dunked kin be." Riffling the clothing of a corpse, he dropped a pearl necklace into his frock pocket. "Fer me it whar a pickled liver that done me in."

"Maybe you should give up drinking." My words had the raspy hoarseness of Clint Eastwood.

"Did give it up. Several times, in fact." He kicked a corpse and knocked loose a silver pendant. "But drinking helps settle me nerves befer I go ter ... *burrrp*, ter work."

"Oh?" I pushed up on my elbows. "And what sort of work do you do?"

"I be a doc ... *bah*, I be a doc ... *burrrp* ..."

"Dock hand?" I suggested.

"Ship's surgeon."

"But you only have one ... you know ..."

"And kin do the work of a feller with two, thank you very much." With his hook, he speared a charm bracelet off a fancily dressed woman.

"What sort of work did you do before you became a surgeon?"

"I used ter be a … *burrrp*, used ter be a … *bah*, used ter be a bar, bar, bartender, but I quit. Ter, ter many, ter many drunks."

"Umm … this ship of yours, is it, you know, nearby? Cause I'd really like to sail back to Mom if that's even possible."

"Oh sure, it's one of those lar, lar, long ones with lots of wooden whatchacallits sticking up."

"Masts?"

"Oh? You a ship's surgeon too?"

"Nope. Just someone trying to, you know, figure out what I did to end up in this place."

"Oh, that's easy. Look out yonder at that graveyard of sunken ships with their masts sticking out of the water. Why, I bet folks on them ships didn't expect to end up here either. The choices we made brought us here."

"But I feel like I'm pretty good. I've never even cheated on a test."

"Not cheating on tests is a good start, but judging from all these bodies lying about—and you and me in this fix—the bar is a good bit higher." He leaned close and whispered, "You know, it be quite a sober … sober, sobering thought and a very inspiring fee … feel, feeling ter know that thar be hundreds of crew and passengers depending … *burrrp,* depending on you ter keep 'em alive while all those big whatchacallits be crashing down on yer ship."

"Waves?"

"Yer sure yer not a ship's doctor?"

"If I was, Mom would be cured of cancer. I'd have made sure of it."

Swinging the jug, he smacked a crab loose from the calf of my leg. "Ave a name, mate?"

"Ricky. Ricky Bradshaw."

"Thomas Tew." *Burrrp.* "Whar the only feller Blackbeard feared. Crew calls me Tew Few on account of I often take a few too many tugs on the jug."

"You served with Blackbeard the pirate?" I asked.

"Aye. Whar Blackbeard's purser, the one who doles out the rum aboard our ship. But we can chat about that later. Fer now, we need ter get you off this beach. Stay on this beach and them crabs 'ill pick you clean. Also, thar not be a tide, but if water laps over yer tootsies, it 'ill burn the skin right off."

I tried to push myself onto my hands and knees but exhausted, I fell back. Waving their pinchers in a threatening manner, more crabs emerged from the water, crawling onto my feet, legs, and arms.

"Take hold of me hook and I 'ill pull you clear."

Swatting crabs away, he pulled me from the tide line and propped me against the stone wall. "Don't go a wanderin' off. I need ter see if that grog shop has any fresh spirits."

"But what about the crabs?"

"They got spirits enough of thar own and of an evil sort."

"Like … deviled crabs?"

"Now you be getting the lay of things, mate."

Without warning, a massive swarm of gulls descended upon the beach, their wings creating a turbulent gust of wind. With relentless determination, they swooped down, pecking at my flesh, their razor-sharp beaks biting my ears. I swatted at the birds, but my blows only seemed to excite them further.

Forced to my feet, I yelled, "Why are the birds attacking us?"

"Payback fer what man done ter all creation. Nature be cursed on account of our wickedness. Wicked spirits hate endin' in the bottomless pit, the place whar ever thing vile churns and burns and whar demons be cast ter await judgment.

Such spirits take delight in possessing a body and any old body 'ill do."

Getting pecked and pinched, I cowered under a palm tree. "So where's the fire? Isn't there supposed to be a fire in the Lake of Hell?"

"This be but the Great Abyss, and if we don't get someplace safe, you 'ill end up like me … down ter but bones. Ter the church, and quick like. Thar not be an evil spirit that would dare inhabit a holy place."

I darted after him, but before I could even take a step, a relentless army of crabs with menacing pinchers crawled onto my feet, legs, and up my thighs. Their sharp pinchers sank deep into my flesh in places I won't mention. Joining the fray, colossal wharf rats emerged from every crevice, every crack in the walls of rotting buildings and boardwalks. With tiny teeth glistening with rat saliva, they surged over me, their numbers overwhelming. The combined assault of the crabs and rats and gulls left me flailing about.

"Mate, don't waste time fighting back. Run!"

Outnumbered, I sprinted, crushing crabs, and leaped a ditch to safety on the bluff. Rats and crabs halted at the edge. Gulls screeched but respected church boundaries. Following Tew Few, we reached the door and collapsed inside. Tew Few slammed it shut, sealing us in.

"So we're safe?" I asked.

"Aye. Unclean spirits kin not abide in the presence of holy righteousness."

From the ceiling rafters, huge wolf spiders fell on us.

"Blast it all!" Tew Few shot to his bony feet. "Must be one of 'em churches whar false teachers and preachers spread lies 'bout Skipper's words and create a welcomed home fer deceiving spirits."

As quickly as I brushed one away, more hairy spiders fell on me.

"Ter the belfry!"

Following Tew Few, we entered the belfry.

He slammed shut the trap door. "That ought to keep out 'em hairy-legged jumpers."

Bats flew from the church bell, attacking us—first one sinking its fangs in my neck, then another.

"We 'ave to jump!"

Stunned, I looked at Tew Few, then at waves bashing against the base of the cliff. "You said the water would burn my skin off."

"No choice, mate."

Bats swarmed, clinging to my bangs, biting my nose and cheek. "No way. Not doing it."

"Stay here and you'll get picked and pecked apart, mate," Tew Few warned.

"Better that than falling into a steaming hot sea."

"Once yer flesh burns off, it won't hurt as much."

"Still not jumping."

Tew Few grabbed my shoulder, urging me to the edge. "We'll jump together."

I shook free and stomped a spider crawling through the trap door.

"Watch. I'll jump first. Show you it ain't so bad."

"No you won't." I pulled him away from the edge. "You're not leaving me to fight these bats alone."

"Then you jump first."

"No way."

"Alright, no jumping," Tew Few said. "It's you that's doing the choosing. You can stay here with the bats, rats, spiders, crabs, and gulls, jump into a scorching sea that 'ill burn off yer skin, or pinch yerself and try'n wake up from this eternal nightmare."

When pinching didn't work, I closed my eyes and fell backward.

CHAPTER FIVE

UNMADE BY MERMAIDS WITH TALL TAIL TROUBLES

A short way outside the surf line, receding waves deposited up all manner of flotsam, a fancy pirate word for trash in the water. Broken carriage wheels, broken carriage seats, bloated horse carcasses, and human corpses floated all around us.

Not wishing to get dragged over the reef a second time, I yelled, "Set coming. Kick hard. Otherwise, we'll get hammered by waves."

Tew Few chuckled. "Hammered? Haven't heard that term since Sir Henry Morgan introduced spiced rum."

"You knew Captain Morgan?"

"My pop sailed with 'em when I were young. Told me all sorts of delicious tales 'bout the chap. Pop also told me that at the end of all things, the sea and land 'ill give up the dead. Everyone 'ill be judged according to thar deeds."

"So if we're swimming in a scalding sea with evil spirits ..."

"It does not bode well fer us, mate."

I surveyed the tops of approaching swells. "When the first wave of the set reaches the reef, it will throw out a huge horseshoe-shaped guillotine lip. If we're not careful, we could get shoved into one of the massive coral polyp holes and held down for who knows how long."

"Down ter one hand, I be givin' it all I got, mate. You go on. I 'ill catch up if I kin."

"No. I'm not leaving you behind. Do you hear me? NO ONE GETS LEFT BEHIND! Kick hard!"

"You kick. I 'ill float." Tew Few rolled over and, floating on his back, somehow retrieved a flask from his frock. "Fer me, it be me missus." He took a sip. "So long as she be praying fer me and hoping I 'ill pull through, I remain alive and kicking."

"That makes no sense at all."

"Only tellin' you how it be, mate." He drained the rest of the flask and tossed it into the water. "Me missus cares little fer my ... *burrrp*, fer my drinkin' and even less fer my snore, snore, loud sawin'. But even with all ... *bwaaaah*, all me ... *bah* ... all me faults, she won' give up on me. That be how come I'm still alive and not a corpse like 'em on that beach."

"But you don't have any skin."

"The flesh counts fer nothing. It's the spirit that be life."

"So you're dead but not all the way dead?"

"Something like that, same as you."

As I feared, the lip of the first wave broke over rocks and peeled into the cove, pounding me down and into a tiny, underwater cave. The problem with drowning when you're dead is that you never die, only suffer the panicked torment of drowning. The deeper I sank, the closer I came to the underwater thermal vents belching toxic sulfur burps, so that was also a problem. Out of breath, flailing and thrashing, I finally clawed my way back to the surface.

Panting, gulping air, I floated toward Tew Few. "Mom," I said, shedding more skin. "She'd refuse to give up on me."

As we cleared the headland, a serene cove unfolded before us. There were no tumultuous waves crashing upon the shore, no grim sight of lifeless bodies adrift. Instead, a tranquil scene greeted our eyes—a collection of massive boulders, some towering like houses, glistening with moisture and emitting a gentle haze of steam.

"Aye, mums kin be like that sometimes," Tew Few replied. "Love you so much they squeeze the stuffing out of you."

Kicking with the current, we floated through a field of colossal rock formations. "Maybe we can climb on one of those rocks and rest."

"Don' lay wagers on it. In these parts, good intentions often leave deep indentations."

"Rog? Oh, Roooog. Over here, sweetie."

Hearing a voice call me by the wrong name—and *sweetie at that*—started my heart racing. There was only one person who called me Rog, and that someone was Becky Nance—the girl in my biology class who thinks my name is Roger. I sort of have a crush on her.

Across the cove, a girl lay on a long, flat rock with her bare back to me. From the waist down, greenish-blue scales covered her backside, her legs—and this was the really awesome part—her wide flipper.

"Look away, mate. She be a siren."

"Siren? Looks like a mermaid to me."

"A siren is a mermaid. One with a wicked spirit. Member how I warned you evil spirits be swarming 'bout? How the flesh counts fer nothing?"

"No."

"Well, I did. That siren's call be but only a temptation ter lure you ter her."

"In that case, I'm definitely swimming over."

"Mate, turn away afore you lose yerself."

After all I'd already been through, getting lost on a beach for a little while with a mermaid seemed like a pretty good idea. Also, at that moment the mermaid started singing. And let's face it, a singing mermaid isn't the sort of thing your average teenage boy is going to turn down.

> *My heart is pierced by Cupid,*
> *I scorn all glittering gold,*
> *Nothing will console my heart,*
> *Until the bones of you I hold.*

"Pay no mind ter her tune."

But her tune was absolutely something I was going to pay a *mind ter*—even if her singing voice did have the low, scary voice quality of Vincent Price on Michael Jackson's popular Halloween tune, "Thriller."

> *Come hither, ye fair lad,*
> *For fortune favors the bold,*
> *Into the depths of the sea, you go,*
> *Where my forbidden heart you shall hold.*

With my gaze still fixed on greenish-blue scales glistening with hot steam, the water erupted around me. Three, six, then more mermaids than I could count swam around and underneath me, frolicking, laughing, splashing me with their wide, flipper tails.

"Mate, kick away! Don' get drawn inter thar snare."

"Snare? What snare? The only thing I see is Becky Nance and some other cheerleaders dressed as mermaids."

"It's a mirage. Thar not real."

As quickly as the school of mermaids had appeared, they dove and vanished. On the long, flat rock, the mermaid slid off, also disappearing underwater.

"Mate. This way. Hurry!"

Kicking and pulling—and now doing so with nothing more than bones—I swam toward the rock where Tew Few sat.

"Mate, behind you. She's got your scent."

My scent ... Becky Nance ... never thought I'd hear those four words in the same sentence.

Head down, long, dark hair trailing behind, the mermaid sliced through the water the way a shark might, her greenish-blue flipper going *hiss, splash* with each pass.

"Mate, grab hold of that rock. Climb up! Get up!"

In my peripheral vision, the sweeps of the mermaid's tail roiled the surface. Thrusting her shapely body up and down, the creature hurtled at me with incredible speed.

"HURRY!"

The mermaid pivoted, rolled onto her side, and splashed me.

"See?" I called. "She's just playing with me."

"She 'ill devour you! She's a man-eater!"

What does he know? Bet that old skeleton never hung out with a mermaid.

Splashing away, the mermaid circled me, the speed of her laps creating a whirlpool. Other mermaids joined her until, at last, the ring of rainbow colors became a blur. Caught in a vortex whirlpool that pulled me down, I kicked and thrashed, but not too hard. I mean, I was surrounded by mermaids.

Then it happened. A net closed around me.

The Natural Resources Defense Council, an environmental advocacy group, estimates that each year over half a million marine animals are killed by something called "ghost nets." You might think ghost nets catch ghosts. You might also believe cows farting cause global warming.

On the verge of panicking—and at that moment panicking would absolutely have been the right move—the net lurched upward. Before I could blink steaming-hot seawater from my eyes, I fell onto the wooden deck of a ship. Only when I landed did I notice that every ounce of flesh had been burned away.

Over my head, gray sails hung in shreds from spars that creaked and moaned. Seaweed clung to netting below spreaders. The eerie ship showed no signs of life, but as luck would have it, there was, and that life belonged to an individual dressed like Errol Flynn in the movie *Captain Blood*.

"Rog?"

"Becky?"

"What are you doing on my boat?"

CHAPTER SIX

BONES, BLAME, AND BICKERING: FIRST LOVE AND FIERCE WINDS

Anyone with an ounce of empathy for someone they love—or at least have a crush on—would be devastated to learn that a person ended up in the realm of the dead. That should have been my reaction to seeing Becky Nance. But then I remembered I was a young male in the throes of adolescence where narcissistic thinking is perfectly normal.

After that, I felt better.

I was also nothing but bones and those scattered about on deck.

"Warned you those mermaids be trouble, mate."

"There'll be time for placing blame later," I replied.

"Rog? You on my boat?" Becky questioned.

Tew Few held up a bone. "Any idear?"

"Make your best guess," I answered.

Sorting bones like they were puzzle pieces, Tew Few asked, "You two know each other?"

"The worst fifteen years of my life," Becky said.

I frowned at her. "But we didn't meet until kindergarten."

"I'm counting my years of therapy to come."

"Did you bring us aboard?" I asked.

"Rog, clearly you have me confused with someone who knows how to fish."

Tew Few asked Becky, "Any idear where this bone goes?"

"Don't know, don't care."

"The foot bone connects to the ... leg bone. Leg bone connects to the ... knee bone," I sang.

"Rog, please stop."

"I'm sorry, did my singing interrupt you interrupting me?"

"Rog is throwing away his talents," Becky said to Tew Few. "He should be the dummy for a ventriloquist."

"You told me once that you get seasick on a pool float," I replied. "How'd you end up on a ship in the realm of the dead?"

"Just like you to mention something I told you in confidence."

Tew Few held up some small bones. "Finger or toe?"

"Go with your gut," I answered.

"If you must know, I'm on this boat because of a dare," Becky said.

"This isn't one of those need-to-know situations, Becky. I was only asking to be polite."

"When have you ever been polite to me?"

"When it never mattered."

Tew Few held up a bigger bone. "Leg or arm?"

"Make your best guess."

"The dare is this little game some of us play sometimes," Becky continued. "I was supposed to call out the name of someone who made an impact, good or bad, in my life. I blurted out, 'Mary Alice Davis.'"

"Who is Mary Alice Davis?"

"New girl from San Francisco who sits with our group at lunch. Or did sit with our group. She outed me."

"Oh."

"Not like *that*, Rog. Ed and I are a couple, remember?"

"Like I could forget. Like everyone in our sophomore class doesn't know that you and Ed *Too Small* are the pair most likely to get married and live happily ever after."

Becky glared at me. "Why do you hate him so much?"

"I don't hate him so much. I hate him just the right amount."

Tew Few placed my pelvic bone where my chest should have been. "This good?"

I shook my head. "Maybe a little lower."

"Mary Alice posted on social media about how I, ah, you know, have a food phobia."

"You … have a food phobia?" I couldn't imagine.

"No, you moron. Mary Alice Davis is spreading lies about me."

Tew Few straightened from his bone sorting. "Me back aches. I need ter take a break. Kin you finish pullin' yerself tergether?"

"How would you like it if some new girl you invited into your inner circle suddenly went around spreading lies about how much you do or do not eat to all your friends?"

"I only have two friends. Alvin and Charley. They've seen me put away a whole pizza, so I'm pretty sure my eating habits are safe."

"Uh, oh. Thar be trouble brewing on the horizon," Tew Few said.

"Mary Alice Davis turned the group—*MY GROUP*—against me."

"What sort of trouble are you seeing?" I asked Tew Few.

"Of a sort we 'ill not likely escape if we don' get under sail soon."

"No way I could face my friends, not after what she said."

"Last time I seen dark clouds roiling and boiling like this I whar stitchin' up a mate who'd lost his nose ring in a fight."

Becky didn't seem to notice no one was listening. "Mom has trouble sleeping sometimes …"

"The chap didn't make it, and that storm liked ter 'ave sent us ter Davy Jones."

"So I took ... you know, some of Mom's tablets," Becky continued in spite of the fact that no one was answering or paying attention.

"A storm?" I asked.

"And not one we 'ill likely recover from," Tew Few stated.

"I'm sorry, Becky, what were you talking about?"

"Pills, Rog, pills. That's how I ended up here."

"Oh, sorry."

"That's it? That's all you've got to say?" Becky stomped her foot.

Even stomping her foot, she looked amazing.

"Give the course ter sail, and the crew 'ill hop to it."

"But the crew is only the three of us," I replied.

"Be more like a short hop."

"Becky, it's your ship. You have a course you want to sail?"

Tew Few shook his head. "Sorry, mate, but I don' trust a lass on the wheel."

"And I don't take orders from anyone. Especially from a chauvinistic, misogynistic drunk who's nothing more than skin and bones without the skin."

"How about you sheet in the foresail," I said to Tew Few. "Becky, you man the helm."

"*I* am not manning anything." Leaning close, Becky whispered, "I blame you for this."

"I thought you might."

Think, Ricky, think. What would Jack Sparrow do? The only thought that came to mind was some nonsensical rambling about bad eggs and me hearties.

"They who sow the wind, reap bad eggs," I said softly. "Come now, gale and prevail, me hearties."

"You know Gail?" Tew Few asked.

"Not Gail. G.A.L.E," I said, "as in a big blow."

"The Gale I know be a big blowhard." Tew Few laughed. "Kin hardly gets a word in edgewise when she's in the room."

I turned back to Becky. "If you could have a do-over with Mary Alice Davis, would you take it?"

"Sometimes you say really dumb stuff, Rog."

A faint breeze ruffled the water next to the ship.

"Well? Would you?"

Tew Few headed to his post. "Mate, I'll take the helm. Heading and course?"

"Becky, before we came aboard were you wearing a mermaid outfit?"

"What do you think? That I'm six?"

Raindrops splatted on the deck. The mainsail, once limp, suddenly bulged, straining against her lines. A blast of white-hot wind suddenly slammed into the ship, rolling her onto the rails.

"You wished fer Gale," Tew Few yelled. "Gale 'as arrived."

With scalding, yellowish water sweeping over us, the vessel shuddered like some enormous sea monster coming alive.

Helping me to my feet, Tew Few said under his breath, "Yer missy don' seem ter care fer you much. What happened 'tween ther two of you?"

"Same thing that happens with every first love." With my bony fingers gripping the spokes of the wheel, I aimed the vessel seaward, and we charged into the teeth of a hellish tempest. "When we started, it was unreal."

"And?"

"Then things got real bad real fast."

CHAPTER SEVEN

IN SEARCH OF JIGGER SAILS, MY NEW MOTTO IS PUT TO THE TEST

A scorching wind blew us along. Each time the ship's bow crashed into a wave, blistering hot spray blasted my bones.

"I 'ave ter hand it ter you, mate. Well you sail after you pray."

"Wouldn't necessarily call what I did back there a prayer. I only spoke some words from a book I remembered reading."

"By talking ter spirits while on the helm, many a feller has kept himself from goin' mad. That be how come the wheel's spindles be called spooks."

"It's spokes," I corrected, "not spooks."

"Spokes, spooks. You say banana, I say Havana."

In the yellow-grayness of the howling gale, hot rain hammered the wooden decks of *The Terminal Torment*. To be honest, I had no idea the name of Becky's ship, and I didn't dare ask. So *The Terminal Torment* was sort of like a made-up name.

"We're carrying too much canvas," I said. "We need to come into the wind so we can sheet in and shorten sail."

"Oh, no, not the dreaded short sheet," Becky said, mocking me.

"Prepare to come into the wind," I said loudly. "Get ready to set the jigger sail. Also the fore-and-aft mainsail."

"We 'ave a jigger sail?" Tew Few asked.

Becky rolled her eyes. "Bet Rog made up the name of that one. He says dumb stuff like that in World History all the time."

"Whar thar be a jigger sail, thar ought ter be strong spirits ter pour inter said jigger."

"Set the sails first, then you can search for spirits," I answered.

"Saying dumb stuff like 'jigger sail' is a gift Rog has."

"That's not true. My gift is letting you borrow my class notes so you can pass tests."

Becky reached for the wheel. "I'll drive the boat. You help the drunk do the thing with the whatever."

"Can you hold this course?"

"Of course, I can hold this course. What is our course?"

"Straight ahead."

"How do you know that we're not sailing into an even worse storm?" Becky asked. "Ever think of that?"

"I'm choosing to take an upbeat attitude about all this." I could fall apart later.

"Like in kindergarten?" she asked.

"That was different. I had high hopes for us back then."

Tew Few returned from doing some stuff with the sails. "Warned you Gale whar a blowhard."

"With any luck, this storm will pass," I said.

"If it's luck yer countin' on, it jest got worse. Look thar off our stern. Thar be but one ship that sails among the blackest of storms with her decks ablaze."

"Do we have any, what-do-you-call-it, oil for that steering wheel?" Becky asked. "It's hard to turn."

"That's because we have too much weather helm," I told her. "We need to adjust course."

"Didn't I suggest that, like, a second ago?" Becky asked.

"Ship like that kin be none other than the *Flying Dutchman*."

"There's no such ship. The *Flying Dutchman* is a made-up myth."

"Ah, that whar you be wrong, mate. The *Dutchman* ne'er makes port and she ne'er burns up."

"If she never makes port, how can anyone know she exists?"

"Because I sailed aboard her, mate, and I tell you true, some dead men *do* tell tales."

"But you just did."

"Take no prisoners. Leave none alive. That be the way of the *Dutchman's* crew."

"Any idea how we can outrun that boat?" Becky asked.

"Ship," I said. "And the move here is to let fly all the canvas. Go big or go home. That's my motto."

"Trust me," Becky yelled above the raging storm, "Rog never goes big. Totally out of character for him."

Tew Few thumbed his eye patch, removing spray and rain. "Sink me! We 'ave been sighted."

"How can you tell?"

"Her gunports be springing open. I count two rows … no, three rows of cannons. We need ter make speed and be quick about it."

From within the knotted fists of dark clouds, a ship of enormous size emerged from the wall of blackness. Reaching out in front of the *Dutchman*, funnels of rain extended downward from anvil clouds. Spinning, bending twisters— three, six, twelve—spewed rain and spray.

"She commands the weather, the *Dutchman* does," Tew Few continued, "and a ruthless tyrant she be."

Looking off our bow, I said, "Run from a fight and find shelter before a storm. That's my new motto."

"And the coward's way," Becky added.

"We'll head for that headland and hook a left. If we can make it there before the *Dutchman* blows us out of the water, we can try to duck out of sight."

"Like they're not going to know which way we went."

"You have a better plan?"

Becky shrugged. "No."

"In that case, we'll go with mine." Taking another check off our stern I got a sinking feeling in the place where my gut should have been. The *Dutchman* looked to be at least a hundred and thirty feet at the waterline. I pivoted back toward Becky. "Pills? Really?"

"At the moment it seemed like a good idea."

"And now?"

"There are some decisions you wish you could take back but can't."

"Oh, I wouldn't be so sure."

CHAPTER EIGHT

WHEN FATE AND ROMANCE COLLIDE WITH A FOOLISH PIRATE'S DESPERATE PLAN

From just above the ship's waterline, three small lights blinked bright for but a moment. Coming from so far away, the flashes had the appearance of a strand of twinkling Christmas lights. In the next moment, the faint echo of *Boom! Boom! Boom!* preceded three cannon balls that sailed overhead. Two struck the water—one to port, the other to starboard—and the third splashed off our bow.

"Those be warning shots, mate. Her crew be showing the accuracy of her gunners. The next volley 'ill find its mark, you may lay ter that."

"In that case, ready about. Hard-alee. Jibe ho!"

"Rog is obsessed with pirate words," Becky said. "Once for our middle school talent show, he sang 'Blow the Man Down' *a cappella*. Wasn't pretty."

I ignored her and looked at Tew Few. "Let's see if we can find a cannon on board. If so, we'll come right at the *Dutchman* and give them a blow."

"A blow?" said Tew Few. "Mate, fightin'? That 'ill only raise thar hackles. I whar thinking we might run up the white flag."

"Surrender? Never."

"Violence only leads to more violence," said Becky. "I've seen you getting pushed around in the halls at school, Rog. Also not pretty."

"Mate, down ter but one good hand, I prefer cowering and pleading fer mercy ter getting cut ter pieces."

"I'm with the bonehead drunk on this one. This is not a war you want to fight."

I was outnumbered. "Fine. I'll go it alone."

"Run up the white flag now and we 'ill only be tortured a little," Tew Few said. "Resist and the crew 'ill start torturing us by pulling out our fingernails."

"Oh no they won't," Becky said. "No one's touching my nails."

Red flashes erupted from the fiery ship, puncturing the mizzen sail and toppling the crow's nest. Another ball crashed into the water behind us.

"That last shot whar meant fer the rudder," said Tew Few. "Her crew means ter disable us. What be yer orders, mate?"

"See if you can find a cannon, musket, pistol—anything we can use to fire back with."

"Sailing along comfortably, we whar, on a broad reach off the coast of Hispaniola when the sky turned black as night," Tew Few said. "Lightning crackled and thunder boomed." It were as if Tew Few hadn't heard my words. "Not more'n a moment later that a sudden gust swept across the water and slammed inter us, rolling *Queen Ann* on her rails."

"I'm sorry, but did we just change topics?"

"Storm off our stern looks ter be same as the one I spied on that day," he replied, "only larger."

Amidst the dark storm clouds, blood-red sails hung from black spars. Masts jutted up from her deck like crosses. And bodies dangled from the masts as if crucified.

"Like you, Stutterin' Stan Standbridge insisted we run with the wind," Tew Few continued. "He hoped ter get clear of the squall and find shelter. Now, my question be this, mate: knowin' the condition of this vessel and crew, you still think resistin' be a good idear?"

Becky answered before I could. "Rog and good ideas are seldom mentioned in the same sentence, so that's a no."

"You know, just once, you could have my back," I said.

"But then I'd be wrong too."

Even on fire, the *Dutchman's* sails remained trimmed, pulling her briskly along under the howling gale. From amidst the black storm, shots—larger than the others and oddly shaped—came hurtling toward us.

"Smoke pots!" Tew Few hollered. "Take cover!"

Burning clods crashed into our ship and exploded. Globs of burning tar belched dark smoke, setting the deck of the *Terrible Torment* ablaze.

"The only way we'll make it through this is to fight back," I said.

"You're right," said Becky.

"Really? I am?"

"No. I was only agreeing with you so you'd stop talking."

"Mate, if captured, we be doomed ter endless punishment. Perhaps it's best to abandon ship while we can."

"You don't know that," I said. "No one knows what happens after we die."

"That whar you be wrong, mate. Seen it with me own eye, I 'ave. Aboard the *Flying Dutchman* thar be torture chambers, dark cells of eternal solitude, vats with glowing hot lava that burns off the flesh. Course in our case we 'ave no flesh ter burn off, but yer missy does."

"I'm not Rog's anything."

"Becky's right," I said. "She and I haven't been a thing since kindergarten."

"And not even then," Becky shot back.

"Aboard that vessel thar be ne'er endin' destruction that goes on and on forever," Tew Few said.

"All that on one ship?"

"Um, hello?" Becky interrupted. "Can we get back to what's important here? Like keeping the grubby hands of pirates off my booty?"

I chuckled. "Look at you making a pirate joke."

"What makes you think I'm joking?"

A cannonball splashed off our port side, creating a muffled *POP!*

"Ha!" Raising my fist I yelled, "You missed!"

"Aiming fer our rudder, mate. Take it out an we be dead in the water."

Emerging ominously from the darkest clouds, the Dutchman revealed its full, haunting profile. Seaweed hung like ghastly tendrils from the spreaders and rigging, casting an eerie presence. Its hull, completely painted in a sinister black hue, ominously mirrored the infernal blaze of its flaming sails. On the bowsprit, a hideous figure with devilish horns and a blood-red cape gazed down.

"Rog, I need to tell you a secret."

"Let me guess. We're sinking."

"We are?" Becky asked.

"I'm saying that's your secret."

"Never, ever try to get on a game show, Rog. You'd make a lousy contestant."

"Mate, if you don' want ter be drawn and quartered, you best do something and be quick about it. I vote we jump ship."

"Like diving into the searing depths of scalding hot water? Are you out of your mind?"

"On the playground that day in kindergarten," said Becky. "I sort of liked the kissing."

I shifted my attention from the menacing profile of *Dutchman* to Becky. "You did?"

"I was hoping you might kiss me again."

"You were?"

"I never told you this, but I had a crush on you in first grade."

My insides yelled, *Whoa, dude!* It was like a gazillion caterpillars suddenly decided to build a cocoon where my stomach had been and have a massive, squirmy party. The long-awaited swapping of saliva with the girl of my dreams was finally, *finally*, *FINALLY* within arm's reach.

If only I had an arm with which to reach.

"And you were right last week to say no when I asked you for your class notes."

"Mate, you need ter run up the white flag, or else everlastin' shame and contempt await us. We 'ill be thrown inter places of darkness whar thar 'ill be weeping and gnashing of teeth and unendin' punishment."

Becky moved closer. "Had it been me, I would have said no to giving up those notes too. And if you refuse to help me this time, I'll understand." She kissed my cheekbone, then whispered, "But I hope you will."

"You still need my class notes?"

"There's still an exam coming up. And if this stupid plan of yours works and we get out of this alive and I wake up from this nightmare, I'll need an A on my final. Otherwise, I might lose my spot on the squad to Mary Alice Davis."

"But you just said you never wanted to step foot into Quiet Cove High ever again."

"All that changes if I put Miss Prissy Pants in her place." Batting eyelashes so hard she could have strained an eyelid muscle, she said, "You get what I'm saying, right?"

If I had a heart inside my rib cage, it would have exploded from my chest.

"The *Dutchman's* bow be near 'bout close enough to ram us in the bum-bum," Tew Few said. "What be yer orders, Cap'n?"

"You liked us kissing?"

"Wasn't bad."

"In that case ... all hands on deck! Tighten the halyards! Release the jib sheets! Trim the mainsail! Adjust the traveler! Secure the boom vang! Keep a keen eye on the telltales!"

"Rog, you have to be the dumbest pirate ever."

"But at least I'm a pirate."

"No, you're simply a boy pretending to be the hero of a story you'll escape."

CHAPTER NINE

Facing the Unexpected and Startling Terrors of the Afterlife

The *Flying Dutchman* shaved passed so close our hulls nearly scraped. Human skulls served as endcaps on spars, some still with flesh hanging off faces.

Amid the crackling of lightning and the explosion of thunder—the wind and rain—that preceded the arrival of the deadly ship, a sudden calm fell upon us. The few sails we flew fell limp. It was as though the *Dutchman* consumed all the air, all energy, all life. I now understood why Tew Few trembled at the mere mention of the ghost ship. A stench, like that of burning flesh, hung in the hot, humid air.

Aboard the *Dutchman,* masts and spars, tattered sails, and deck crackled with flames, and yet not a single timber appeared consumed by the blaze. Heaps of bodies lay on her deck. Crowded around the piles, zombie pirates brandished barbed clubs and swung chains, each prodding at corpses in the way someone might poke the logs of a campfire.

From within the crackling of fire came moaning, groaning, and screaming.

Huddled under a fallen sail on deck, Becky trembled. "How come they haven't fired at us?"

"Do you hear voices?" I asked under my breath. "I hear voices."

"Could be they wish ter capture the ship whole so as ter put it in thar fleet."

"I'm not letting a bunch of pirates take my boat."

"If they want this ship, they 'ill take it," Tew Few replied. "Crew of the *Flying Dutchman* takes what they want and leaves destruction in their wake."

"I'm telling you two, I hear people talking," I said. "Or rather arguing and screaming."

"If you 'ave ears ter hear, listen. Could be those souls of the dead doomed fer eternal destruction be calling out ter you."

My sweet lord, Krishna Krishna, promised that when I died, I'd come back to a higher state. Now, look at me. I'M A COW!

I dared to rise up on boney elbows and peek. A cow had, in fact, appeared at the *Dutchman's* railing, though not a large cow. More like a calf.

I was a highly respected journalist for National Public Radio. Thousands knew my voice and started their day listening to me report the news. Now I'm a cow? How'd that happen?

"Ah, is it just me, or do you see a baby cow at the ship's railing?" I asked.

"This is how it starts," Becky said to Tew Few. "First come the hallucinations, then the paranoia, followed by the belief that everyone is out to get him."

"I'm not crazy. I know what I see."

"I'm not saying you don't see what you see, Rog. Just pointing out that what you're seeing is not there."

A woman's face appeared next to the face of the baby cow. Her hair was on fire, leaving the lower half of her scalp exposed with only charred skin and her ears blackened, scorched, and curled like leaves consumed by a raging forest fire. *My boyfriend promised that taking pills would be painless, like falling asleep forever. But there is no peaceful, easy feeling. No pleasant ever after. Now his voice keeps whispering in my ear that we will never be together again.*

"You really don't hear people talking?" I asked.

"You asked befer if I really served aboard the *Flying Dutchman*," Tew Few said. "What yer hearing be the reason I jumped ship. The never-ending harvesting of souls and thar constant screamin' and complain' whar more'n I could handle."

"How come you don't hear them now?"

"The longer it went on, the less I cared. And the less I cared, the less I heard 'em. Those lost souls be headed fer eternal destruction whar thar be eternal torment, endless floating in fire, flesh burned with brimstone, unquenchable thirst, total separation from all that be good and those we love, darkness of a sort that leads ter interminable despair and solitude."

Another man joined the baby cow and the woman with her hair on fire.

The baby cow shouted, *Hey, I know you. You're Tom Harrison, the famous atheist and podcaster. I have your book, "The Sole Unifying Factor Among Us is Our Mortality." Can I get your autograph?*

The burning-hair woman interrupted. *You claimed there is no heaven or hell, that the afterlife is only a fairy tale for people afraid of the dark. I believed you. I watched your videos. Now look at me. My hair's on fire!*

I turned to Tew Few. "You really don't hear or see them?"

"Those who 'ave eyes ter see, see. Others turn a blind eye ter the sufferin' all 'round us." Tew Few leaned closer. "You 'ill feel better once you turn away and clap yer hands over yer ears."

"Rog, you need to watch this."

I looked to where Becky pointed. Directly below the *Dutchman*'s railing, a dismembered hand wrote:

> SIRENDER AN YU WILL ONELY SUFER SUM
> REFEWS TWO SIRENDER, AN YU
> WILL GET BLASDED TWO BITS

"Handwritin' on the wall, mate. Or in this case, on the hull."

"Oh, so *now* you see the ghosts?" I replied.

"Hand-me-down hands 'ill sometimes show thar hands," Tew Few explained.

The hand moved to the next plank below and continued writing.

> LAST CHANGE
> RUN UP THE WHTIE FLOG OR ...
> OR GO TO DAVEE JOANS

"You want to know what I see?" Becky asked. "I'll tell you what I see. I see the need for a proofreader."

"What be yer plan, mate?"

Jumping from under the pile of sails, I shouted, "Surrender? Never!"

"Getting 'em riled up whar not the plan I had in mind, mate."

"Sometimes you just have to stand up to a bully," I replied. "Otherwise they will keep—"

KaBOOM!

CHAPTER TEN

THE RISKS OF KEEPING YOUR HEAD WHEN OTHERS LOSE THEIRS

In hindsight, I realize now how my careless challenge must have sounded to the demon spirits who were pointing cannons at us. To the crew, they have a ship in their sights that they think might be filled with dead people who are ready to give up the ghost. But they don't see a soul stirring. Then all of a sudden a skeleton jumps up, shouting and waving his bony arms and yelling, "Surrender? Never!"

It could arouse suspicion. I can see that now.

"Mate, what whar you thinking, yellin' such foolishness?"

"Let's not focus on past mistakes and place blame. What's done is done. We need to see if we can save this ship."

"I'd be content with finding my makeup kit," Becky said. "I had it in my purse. But thanks to you, everything I own is scattered to who knows where."

We crawled from under the shredded sail and stood perched at the edge of a huge crater where most of the main deck had been moments before. With *Terrible Torment* in shambles—its mast fallen over, sails shredded, large holes in the hull, and a really big hole in the deck—the *Dutchman* sailed on, leaving us to sink.

"Be odd that her crew didn't come aboard ter check fer bodies. Especially when you yelled such nonsense."

Locating a sharp axe in the place where sharp axes are kept, I hacked away the mainmast and rigging. "Give me a hand. The more we can lessen the load, the better."

Tew Few joined in, his strikes joining mine in a symphony of destruction. With each blow, the rigging weakened, and the mast shifted perilously close to the side of the ship.

"Even the bones of two be worth a wee little bit. Thar must be a reason they left us afloat."

"Speaking of uttering nonsense, what happened to your stuttering from earlier?"

"Oh, that only hap, hap … occurs when I be drinking. Or right this moment when I be put, put, 'ave ter give an account of me actions."

"Becky? Maybe you could help?"

She continued searching among the debris for her makeup kit. "Or not."

Dank, muggy air filled with the odor of decaying bodies mingled with insufferable, sweltering heat. All the while, thunder boomed, howling wind whipped up white caps, and lightning flashed within the roiling clouds.

"Supposin' we do cut away the wreckage an' keep us afloat. You 'ave a plan fer what ter do next?"

With one last unified swing, the remaining strands of rigging snapped. The mast skidded toward the side of the ship closest to the water. Teetering on the edge, we only needed to give it a hard shove to send it over, but if you've ever tried to push a downed tree even a little, you know how hard that can be.

"Ah, um … think we should follow that ship," I answered.

"But, mate, we be sinking."

With a grunt of great effort, we shoved and the mast fell over, crashing into the steamy hot sea with a thunderous splash that showered up in a steamy hot spray.

"And now without a mast, the prudent skipper would make way fer a safe harbor."

Becky looked up from her search. "And Rog is nowhere near prudent—or even a skipper."

"Are you sure you had a makeup kit?" I asked her. "Perhaps you only think you had it."

"Seriously, Rog. If you want to remain on my boat, you need to stop saying stupid stuff."

With the mast gone, we set about sawing other spars into smaller pieces that we could roll off.

"If the *Flying Dutchman* is carrying souls," I said, "eventually she will have to drop off her cargo, right?"

"Suppose so. I ne'er stuck 'round long enough fer her ter make port."

"And when the *Dutchman* drops off cargo, some person or spirit or whatever will check in said cargo, right?"

"Could be … I suppose," Tew Few answered.

"And if said someone or spirit is entrusted with logging in said cargo, then doesn't it stand to reason that they would have access to the full inventory of all souls received heretofore? And the names of those about to be heretofore received?"

"Mate, you lost me among all 'em heretofers. Jest state plain yer intentions."

"Save Mom, save us, and get back to someplace with A/C."

"Mate, the *Flying Dutchman* makes port at The Isle of Abaddon whar lost souls be tossed inter such a fierce, blazing furnace that thar weeping and gnashing teeth only be drowned out by thar horrifying screams. You sail after her, that be whar we 'ill end up."

"Found it!" Becky held up a charred, leather ear—or so it appeared. "My makeup kit." She pried open a flap. "Oh, that's just great. My Chanel Rouge Intense Luminous Lip Colour has melted. There goes sixty dollars I'll never get back. Good job, Rog."

As the sound of wood cracking and snapping mingled with Becky's complaining, splinters flew through the air. Tew Few and I whacked and hacked and sawed with the effort of two lumberjacks competing in the Highland Games.

"Selfish, greedy, hateful, murdering, rebellious, grumbling, faultfinders be all about on The Isle of Abaddon. You sure it be wise ter sail ter such a wicked port?"

"Of course, it's not wise." Becky dusted her cheek with a brush sprouting only three bristles. "It's Rog we're talking about."

"Way I see it, we only have two options," I answered. "Do something or do nothing."

"If we're going to go anywhere, I say we head for a beachfront resort or spa, showers, and guest suites large enough that I can spread out without the two of you in my face all the time."

"Mate, we 'ave a wee bit of wind and maybe the current as well. If we could reach that headland you mentioned earlier, perhaps we could float ter shore. But someone 'ill need to man the pumps."

Straining to see where I'd last spotted the headland, I said, "Is that someone out there in the water?"

"A corpse from the *Dutchman*, most likely," Tew Few said.

"But what is it doing out there," asked Becky.

"Floating?"

Becky snickered a little at my joke.

Wow! It's official. She likes me.

"Probably tumbled off a burnin' pile without any of thar *Flying Dutchman's* crew noticin'."

"But why is that person waving at us?" I asked.

"And why doesn't he have a head?" Becky added.

The person waving at us was, in fact, missing a head.

"Drop sails!" I shouted. "Deploy rope ladders! Let loose lines! Prepare to bring survivors aboard!"

"Power 'as gone ter his head," Tew Few said. "Happens ter the best of 'em."

"And Rog is nowhere near the best of them," Becky replied.

"Come on, you two. If you were a headless person floating in hot water, wouldn't you want to be taken aboard?"

"First off," Becky said, "I'd never lose my head. That's why I'm the head cheerleader."

"Mate, sails be dropped all about the deck. Lines loosed as well. But …"

At my insistence, Tew Few tossed a line over.

"And second, no," Becky said.

"No?"

"Who wants to be pulled aboard a sinking boat, Rog?"

"Ship. Ship. This is a *ship*!"

"Fished 'em out, mate. Though from the looks of 'im, he's not much of a catch."

Holding his decapitated head on his hip, the disheveled man's eyes looked about as if confused.

"Snake?" I asked.

"Bradshaw?"

"You know this chap?" Tew Few asked.

"Bossman said heads would roll, you weaseling, backstabbing, stiff! And so they did, starting with mine. But if I have my way, yours will be next!"

CHAPTER ELEVEN

HEADS WE LOSE, DEBTS WE OWE, AND THE CURSE OF FIRST LOVE

"You know this headless chap?" Tew Few asked again.

Tripping over lines and broken spars, Snake called, "Where are you, you lying stiff?"

"Sort of," I replied. "But do you ever really know someone?"

"I wish you'd stop bringing her up."

Hiding behind Tew Few, I said to Becky, "Who?"

"Mary Alice Davis, that's who."

"I was only making the point that it's really hard to know someone."

Becky shot back, "Oh, so now it's my fault that all my friends have turned on me."

Snake's narrow face, large eyes, and scruffy bits of whiskers growing from his bony chin gave him a comical look, even for a headless person. "You reneged on the deal, you double-crossing stiff."

"Sorry, Snake."

"Sorry is as sorry does."

"What's that supposed to mean?" I manned one of the pumps on deck. Though I could not see down into the bilge from the way the ship leaned, I knew water was rushing in below.

"No idea," Snake answered. "I heard a constable in Port Charles say it to an old sot who was pleading for his life. I always wanted to say it to someone."

Gripping the lever firmly—and with a forceful pull—I drew water up, repeating the process until water spewed from a pipe over the side.

A few feet from me, with one hand and a hook, Tew Few proved quite the man-overboard boatswain. "Fished up one more, mate." Like Snake, this man also appeared filthy and unshaven.

Fighting against the relentless flood gushing in, I became caught up in this repetitive cycle of pushing and pulling. "Hey, Will." It became clear that I had to keep up the pace or we'd sink— and soon.

"That's Clean Willie to you, you lying, weaseling, backstabbing stiff."

"Why do they keep calling you a stiff, mate?"

"Back in Port Charles, we lugged this ungrateful stiff to the harbor," Clean Willie interrupted. "The crew of the *Flying Dutchman* was to take ownership of his body. Now look at you. Same as before. Same as it ever was. Let's all twist our thumbs. Here comes the twister."

Snake joined in, singing a familiar tune, "letting the days go by, water flowing all around."

Taking a quick breather, I said, "Talking Heads?"

"Snagged one more, mate."

Clinging to the end of Tew Few's rope, a shirtless man wearing a butcher's apron advertising EARL THE BUTCHER'S BUTCHER SHOP flopped over the railing.

"Stab me again with that hook and I 'ill gut ya like a grouper."

The last of the survivors wore grubby black boots and a scowl to match his unkempt appearance.

"Jest you try it, fatso," Tew Few shot back.

Pause over, I returned to pumping. "Now, boys, let's not get off on the wrong foot."

"Ya and Bones McSkinny don't have a foot ter get off on." Earl the Butcher wiped grubby hands on bloodstained pants. "Get it? No footsies?"

Becky walked over. "I'm going below to pack my things."

"You're leaving?"

"As soon as my ride arrives."

"Hey, stiff, I 'ave bounty papers on ya," said Earl the Butcher.

"Before you go," I said to Becky between grunts, "in kindergarten, on the playground, right after we met, why did you kiss me?"

"I wanted to see how it felt," Becky answered.

As though wiping sweat from my brow, I brushed away hot, steamy sea mist from the top half of my skull. "And?"

"Some things are better left unknown."

Over my shoulder, I called, "You have bounty papers on me?"

"Aye. And of a kind that put ya in debt ter a nefarious crew of pirates who be none ter pleased that you stiffed 'em, stiff." Rummaging through his apron pockets, he pulled out a wet clump of paper that looked as if it could have once been a parchment scroll. "The ink ran sumpin' terrible due ter me being in the sea a wee little bit, but the document still be legally binding."

Tew Few asked, "You know this chubby nubby?"

"Only in passing," I answered.

"Only in passing." Snake snickered. "Gotta remember that one."

"Like I splained back in Port Charles," Earl said, "a ship's cargo cannot back out of a deal. Sends a bad message ter other cadavers and inter-the-depths divers."

"I didn't back out of any deal." Backing away from the pump, I took a seat on what remained of the main's boom. "There was no deal to back out of."

"Papers on ya say otherwise." From the front pocket of his apron, Earl pulled an assortment of body parts: a thumb, a toe, a fistful of teeth … a mangled ear. "Ah, here 'tis." He unfolded a crumpled piece of paper.

"Uh, oh. I smell trouble," said Tew Few.

"That's Snake," Clean Willie said. "Rotten flesh around his neck stinks something terrible when it starts to dry."

"Ter the person or persons in possession of said cargo," Earl read loudly, "be it hereby resolved this Ricky Bradshaw has released all rights ter the Sergeant of Arms aboard the *Flying Dutchman* in exchange fer … and then I can't read the rest. Ter much blood on it."

"It don' stink like decaying flesh," Tew Few interrupted. "But reeks more along the lines of trouble of a treacherous sort."

Earl waved the paper in front of my face. "Ya owe double on account of ya stiffed me back in Port Charles."

"Stiffed me." Snake snickered again. "Good one, Boss."

"Furl yer flap, Snake."

"This trouble you're smelling …" I jumped back into action, ready to save the day—or at least save us from being cast into hot water. "Can you be more specific?"

"Hard ter know," Tew Few replied. "But it be in the wind, you may lay ter that."

"Second off, that stunt of yers cost me a pretty six pint."

"Don't you mean it set you back a pretty six pence, Boss?"

"Warning you, Snake. Ya don't keep quiet, I 'ill sell yer head ter a haberdasher hat shop."

"Boss," Clean Willie whispered, "haberdasher and hat shop be mostly the same thing."

Balling up his fist Earl said, "Ya want some of this?"

"We never had a deal," I argued. "You only had a slip of paper with an X for my signature."

"Still legal. Ya owe the crew of the *Flying Dutchman* one body in good condition." Earl paused, surveying my skeleton. "And down ter bare bones, like ya be, yer not worth near what ya once whar."

"Bare bones." Snake giggled. "Boss, you crack me up."

"And cracked up 'ill be yer skull if ya don't clap that trap of yers."

"Not another word, swear it." Snake puckered his lips, causing his narrow, shriveled face to pinch worse than before.

Glancing about, and still no sign of Becky, I grew worried. Like, maybe she'd fallen into the ship's hold that was now filling with water and was drowning. "Hold that charge. I have to go check on something."

"You can't leave. I be in the middle of makin' accusations."

"It's not like I'm going to run away on a sinking ship."

One deck below I found a wide, open area that might have once been used for sleeping and firing cannons. Now, with most of its flooring gone, the space was but an open crater. In a hallway I went about opening doors, peering into darkened nooks and craning into crannies. In the galley—a fancy sailing word for *kitchen*— beams, skillets, and pots dangled by handles. A meat cleaver with dried blood on its blade lay on a cutting board.

"Find anything interesting?"

Becky appeared behind me dressed in her Quiet Cove JV cheerleader's outfit.

"You ... you changed out of your pirate outfit and into your uniform? How's that possible?"

"Oh, please. You don't think I'd take a trip like this without packing an overnight bag, do you?"

I knew better than to comment on what a girl does or does not pack for a trip, so I said nothing.

"I wouldn't be caught dead traveling without gum or mints, a toothbrush and floss, tissues, pens, glasses, sunglasses, phone charger, hair bands, bobby pins, nail file, personal things, Advil, lotion, granola bars, lip balm, cozies, and a Starbucks gift card."

"You packed all that?"

Becky twisted the end of her ponytail. "You never answered before about how you ended up on my boat?"

"Ship. And it's actually sort of funny and sad at the same time. See, Mom has stage-four cancer and—"

"Rog, I was only asking so you would ask me how I ended up on this boat."

"Oh, okay. How did you?"

"I'd rather not go into it."

"But you just said ..." Hearing myself about to make a point that I would certainly pay for later, I slammed on the brain brakes. "You wouldn't happen to have a pair of shorts and a shirt that would fit me, would you?"

"People think if you're popular and have parents who can afford to live on a golf course, that you have an easy life, but it's not like that. Those with less can be just as judgmental as I am. Wait, that didn't come out right."

"I got it. And I don't think you're judgmental at all."

"It's like tearing me down makes them feel better, I guess. I mean, you hang out with Alvin and Charley and other dorky boys who are probably going to run the world, but can't get a date, so you probably can't really relate to what I was going through."

I had no idea what she meant, but I said, "Probably not."

"I begged Mary Alice to stop posting about me. Told her I'd go to our guidance counselor if she didn't. I bet you can guess what she did next."

Again, no idea, not a clue, but I nodded as if I did.

"Mary Alice told all the girls at my table that I was seeing a therapist because of my depression. Me? Depressed? Seriously?

She's the one who's a mental case. Honestly, some days I hate high school."

"A lot of days I hate high school too."

"Rog, stop interrupting when we're talking about me."

"So, did the counselor bring you and Mary Alice into her office so you could work things out?"

"Clearly, you have no idea how screwed up mental health counseling is in public schools."

Clearly.

"Of course, the counselor took Mary Alice's side."

Of course.

"So I went home, raided my mother's medicine cabinet, and went out to sit by our pool. That's how I ended up here on this boat." Becky snuggled up close. So close I could smell the minty flavor of ALTOIDS on her breath. "I need you to fix this."

"Fix this?"

"So I can get back at Mary Alice Davis."

Head: *Help Becky get back at Mary Alice Davis? That would require me bringing her back from the almost-dead. How am I going to do that?*

Heart: *Might score some points with Becky. You should go for it.*

Head: *But I'd need a crazy plan.*

Heart: *You've done dumber things.*

Head: *You mean like getting baptized by a pirate preacher?*

I could almost hear smart aleck, logical Ricky snickering at me.

"I know I'm going to get shot down for asking, but here goes. If I'm able to undo what can't be undone, do you think there's any chance at all of the two of us ever becoming a couple?"

"There you go speaking in riddles again. Use plain English, Rog."

"Is there a chance the two of us might, you know, one day, like, be able to maybe, I don't know, hang out?"

"A chance? Well, I suppose there's always a chance."

"In that case, I'm definitely down for possibly—"

"All hands on deck," Earl called down. "All hands on deck. That means you, stiff."

CHAPTER TWELVE

FROM LOVE BOAT TO BOUNTY BLUES AND A SHIPWRECKED ROMANCE

"Ya owe me a body. Two in fact. One ter replace the corpse ya took at Port Charles. Another ter settle the interest fer ya keepin' it fer so long," Earl demanded.

On deck, the shattered planks of the *Terrible Torment* appeared even worse than before. While sinking, the ship appeared to be imploding.

"But it was my body to start with," I protested.

"Which ya deeded ter the Sergeant of Arms aboard the *Flying Dutchman*. A deal's a deal."

The stench of sulfur water smelling like rotten eggs mingled with the not-so-fresh odor of three unwashed bounty hunters.

Tew Few leaned close. "Mate, yer not goin' ter like what I be about ter say."

I kept my eyes on Earl. "I never agreed to any deal."

"I beg ter dither."

"Ey, Boss," said Clean Willie. "It's I beg to differ."

Earl the Butcher balled his fist. "And I say dither!" Earl boxed Will's ear.

"OW!"

Wincing, Clean Willie grabbed his ear. "How come you never hit Snake like —"

Earl hit Will's other ear.

"OW!"

"Stop repeating yerself, Will. It be tiresome."

With each sloshing groan of the sinking vessel, my unformed plans for getting Becky back to the land of the living sank a little more.

Pulling a scroll from the front pouch of his bloody apron, Earl unfurled it and read.

STOLEN CARGO!

REWARD OFFERED!

WANTED DEAD OR ALIVE

DEAD PREFERRED

See the Sergeant of Arms aboard the
Flying Dutchman for Your Reward.

Below the copy was a crudely drawn sketch of a face—and that face was mine.

I turned to Snake. "Did you draw this?"

Snake, looking embarrassed, tucked one foot behind the other.

"It's actually pretty good," I said. "Mind if I keep it?"

Tew Few tried to get my attention. "Mate, it be terribly important that I 'ave a word with you. It's about what be about ter come next."

Snatching the poster from me, Earl said, "Official papers remain with official persons."

"So technically I'm a wanted man?"

Becky appeared on deck with a soft luggage bag. "*Man* is a reach."

Apparently, our almost-a-couple status had slipped a notch.

"And there's about as much water in this boat as there is around it," Becky continued.

"SHIP!" the rest of us shouted in unison.

"There be a bounty on yer head and I aim ter cash in," said Earl. "Hands behind yer back. Yer under arrears."

"Boss, I think you mean arrest," said Snake.

"Arrears be a debt owed," Earl said, showing a level of intelligence I did not think he possessed. "And this stiff should've thought about payin' his be fer now."

"Mighty important, mate. More'n important than this banter, of that you kin be sure."

"We're sinking into hot water, you and I are only bones, and I'm about to be arrested for something I didn't do. How can it be more important than this?"

"I say what I mean and mean what I say," Earl interrupted, "and I say a nice bounty be coming my way."

Tew Few hobbled over to where Becky stood frowning into a makeup mirror. "He don' seem ter care, but you might. I spy sails on the horizon. Two points ... no three points off our stern."

"Use words that someone not in a *Pirates of the Caribbean* movie might," Becky shot back.

"A ship, missy. A big one is approachin'."

Hearing the word *ship,* I looked to where the pair stared. On the rim of the yellowish-brown horizon, first one white sail, then a second appeared.

"Rog, he's right. There's a boat of some kind out there."

"SHIP!" we all yelled.

"Boat be smaller and used fer recreation," said Earl.

"Like I care."

"You 'ill care when ya find out what sort of vessel she be."

"Sail ho!" Snake had lifted his head high in his hands so he could see across the water. "Sail ho! Sail ho!"

"We're not blind," Clean Willie said. "We see the sails."

Off the starboard side, the top half of two more masts appeared on the rim of the hot, hazy sea.

"And another vessel," Tew Few announced. "Two-masted and comin' from … *abeam*."

"Sail ho!" Snake swung his head back and forth as if he were swinging a lantern to warn of danger. "Sail ho!"

"STOP YELLING IN MY EAR!" Becky shouted.

"Comin' from that aft, she not likely ter be the *Flying Dutchman*," Tew Few said.

"One vessel astern, another ter starboard, and now"—Tew Few adjusted his eye patch—

"one ter port." With his bony hand on my shoulder blade, he tried to comfort me. "Mate, with the *Flying Dutchman* somewhere off our bow, I fear you 'ave sailed us inter a trap."

"But you were on the helm when we were attacked," I replied.

"Under yer orders."

"You're right. This is on me. It's always the captain's fault. Even when it's not."

"Time ter vote fer a new skipper," Earl said.

"Hang on. Before we vote on a new captain, isn't someone supposed to give me the black spot? I mean, aren't there rules about this sort of thing?"

"You 'ave sort of sailed us onter a lee shore." Tew Few slipped off his eye patch and placed it in my palm.

"There, Bones McSkinny agrees with me."

"I didn' say I whar votin' fer you, Chubby Nubby."

"Will? Snake? What says ya?"

"Boss man forever," Clean Willie said.

"Boss man forever," said Snake with less enthusiasm.

"Only need one more fer a majority." Earl leaned toward Becky. "How 'bout ya, lassie? Cast yer lot with old Earl?"

"Drop dead."

Snickering, Snake said, "Drop dead, that's a good one."

Earl slapped Snake's head out of his hand, sending it rolling onto the deck.

"Before we vote," I said, "I need to know how the three of you *ended up in the water.*"

Snake, bending down to pick up his head, mumbled, "Can't talk about it. Sworn to secrecy."

"Will?"

"What Snake said."

"Are we going to vote or not?" asked Becky. "I need to do my nails before my ride arrives."

"You want a new captain?" I asked. "Fine."

"Snake, run up the white flag."

"Hang on," I said. "Don't we have to vote?"

"Changed my mind," said Becky. "I say we make chubby grubby captain of my boat."

"Ship," Earl corrected.

"You want my vote or not?" Becky asked.

"Boat it is," said Earl.

Snake asked, "Run up the flag on what, Boss? All the masts are down."

"Just wave sumpin' white. Anything 'ill do. That 'ill let the crew of the *Flying Dutchman* know old Earl be in control of the vessel."

"Will, cuff these two sacks of bones. Snake, you get a gig ready so we can ferry the pair over ter the *Dutchman* when she arrives. I 'ill go write up some papers ter let the Sergeant of Arms know I caught his escaped cargo and that I 'ill be expectin' a reward with a bonus."

"What about the stiff's missy?" Clean Willie asked. "You want her cuffed and shipped over as well?"

"Missy? Me with Rog?"

"No need," Earl answered. "The lass held up her end of the bargain. She delivered this lying, deal-reneging scoundrel as promised."

I wheeled to face Becky. "Really? You turned me in?"

"Survival of the fitness."

"It's fittest," I replied.

"You say fittest, I say fitness, but which of us is fit to be tied now, umm?"

"But a little bit ago you asked me to help fix things between you and whats-her-name."

"Had to cover my bases, Rog. Wasn't sure you could come through. Like those class notes you never gave me."

Tew Few mumbled, "Love be a fickle thing."

"Shut up."

"Speaking of things what be up," Earl said. "Yer time be up, stiff. Get ready ter give the Devil what's due."

CHAPTER THIRTEEN

GRAVE BARGAINS, SKELETONS IN CLOSETS, AND HAGGLING IN THE UNDERWORLD

Squashed and defeated like the *Terrible Torment*, that's how I felt. How could I have been so stupid? I wanted to crawl into a storage closet with a sign over it that read, *Beware of First Love Crushes.*

Hold on, Captain All-Too-Serious. Let's take a moment to reflect. Becky never actually said the two of you could be a couple. She only hinted at it. And you should know that Becky is all about Becky. Then again, you're all about you.

Whose side are you on? Mine or hers.

Careful, big guy. Don't forget that you don't have a brain. This internal bantering could flip a switch and send you back to—

"The *Dutchman's* Sergeant of Arms will see you now." A gruff-looking pirate with the stiff, rigid gait of a zombie pushed open a door. "Or see as much of you as there is to see."

"You should be one to talk."

The Sergeant of Arms sat behind a wooden desk. Nostril hair joined the whiskered fur of a mustache that obscured his upper lip. A pair of earrings fashioned from bits of bone dangled from both lobes. Though his expression appeared almost completely hidden by long, oily hair, small eyes shimmered like black diamonds in the candle's flame. You might think that I would get accustomed to the stench of rotting body parts filling rooms on underworld ships, but this putrid odor of decomposing flesh had a particularly tart smelliness.

The little man removed a wedding band from a hand. "MBC to REJ. Fourteen karat and of good quality." With a casual flip of his wrist, he pitched the hand onto a pile of body parts and pocketed the ring. Without looking up he asked, "Don't suppose you have a flask of cold water on you?"

"Sorry, fresh out," I replied.

A single, oval window along the room's back wall revealed flashes of lightning.

"Figured as much. Doesn't hurt to ask." Fixing his gaze on me for the first time he said, "Where is your body?"

"Not sure. I had it with me when I left home."

Peals of thunder shook the floor beneath my bony feet.

"Sarcasm will earn you demerits. This not be the sort of place where you wish to have points removed." He lifted a quill from its well, hovering its tip over a page in a ledger. "Name?"

"Ricky. Ricky Bradshaw."

Rotating in his chair, he pulled a large leather-bound volume from a bookcase and flipped pages. "Brad ... Brads ... Bradsh ..." he murmured. "Ah, here we go. Date of death?"

"I'm, ah, not exactly sure. It's possible I might not be dead."

"Best guess will be fine. Accounting department will do a full audit later."

I tried to count back to when Mom and I had left to see the pirate preacher, but having lost all concept of time, I couldn't be exactly sure.

"Today, mid-morning, I think."

"We'll fix it at ten a.m. Reason for death?"

"A baptism went wrong."

This elicited a stern look. "Doesn't appear it did you much good."

On a shelf next to his desk a leather-bound book spewed smoke, shuddered, then tipped forward.

"Ah, um, one of your books is moving," I said.

Sarge glanced over his shoulder and then back at me. "Inspired works by egocentric authors can be especially bothersome."

The book flopped off the shelf, landing with a loud clunk. Tendrils of dark mist wafted upward from the pages.

"An author pours so much of herself into a book," Sarge continued, "that she thinks she is entitled to special treatment."

Within a dark, misty haze, the round face of a woman took shape.

"Yes, Anna, what is it?"

The ghostlike face emerged from the book, moaning. Her pudgy cheeks grew even fatter. Though I could not read her lips, the small man seemed to perfectly understand what the ghost was saying.

"You will know when I know, and you won't know before I know," Sarge said to the ghost. "But I told you, you have to be patient. These things take time." Then Sarge whispered to me, "Some days this job is pure hell."

"Why not quit?" I asked.

"And give up all this? Inside work? A desk job? Plus, I'm almost vested in the retirement program. Reach the magic date and I can cut back to half-time work."

"How many more years?" I asked.

"No idea. The Keeper of Days continues to change my retirement date."

Wispy tendrils curled upward from Anna the author, forming a nest of venomous snakes that closely resembled Medusa on a bad hair day. Sarge rolled his chair back to keep out of range of the illusionary snakes.

"Yes, Anna, I know you hate them. Everyone aboard knows you hate them and wish them dead."

"Wish who dead?"

"Book reviewers. Authors loathe them. Especially amateurs who couldn't spell *loathe* if their life depended on it. Anna remains convinced *Ferg* would have become a young adult best seller if it had not received so many one-star reviews."

"Oh."

"Her first page is actually pretty good, but the tale goes downhill from there."

"I read a lot, and I've never heard of *Ferg.*"

"Few have. For a writer, obscurity is pure hell."

Anna's dark vapor swelled to the size of a balloon about to pop.

"Speaking ill of the dead will not change your book's reputation," Sarge said to the ghost. "Were I you, I'd be grateful no one hardly remembers you wrote a book at all."

The author's misty shape expanded, morphing into the shape of a dust devil. Spinning about, the mini tornado hopped through the room, scattering hands and arms and small digits that had been sorted by size and use.

"That's it. Out!" At the snap of his fingers, the window along the back wall flew open. A vacuum of air sucked Anna out and into the black tempest that engulfed the *Dutchman.*

Another snap and the window shut. "Mark my word, she'll be back soon enough begging to be let in." Returning his attention to the large book on his desk, he mumbled, "Um … says here you owe a debt of gratitude. Something about claiming a body that didn't belong to you. Know anything about that?"

I recounted the whole business with Earl the Butcher, Snake, and Clean Willie and how I had retrieved my body at the sea wall in Port Charles.

"Body snatching is a capital offense in these parts, punishable by death."

"But I'm already dead. Or almost."

"I'm speaking of the second death, the never-ending death that never ends. Very painful, it is. Eternal torment. The way you pass is the way you die forever. In your case, it will be endless drowning. No amount of struggling will ever bring relief. For others, it is the sharp, intense pain of a sword or musket ball passing through organs and tissue. Horrible, it is, the second death. Not a thing to be wished upon by anyone." Refocusing his attention on me, he asked, "For this case, do you have a barrister representing you?"

"Ah, no. Do you think I need one?"

"These are serious charges. For stealing a corpse, you will need to provide one body. To cover the fine of theft and its associated court costs, you will need a second body."

"But the body I took was my own."

"A trivial fact that matters not at all." He looked me up and down. "I can give you twenty-five cents on the dollar and no more."

"Twenty-five cents? That's crazy. My frame is already put together. No assembly is required. That has to be worth something."

"And it is. Twenty-five cents. That's my final offer, take it or leave it."

I thought about saying, "Leave it," but on a ship filled with spirits, I wondered where I would leave to—out the window like author Anna and into the scalding hot sea?

"Where am I possibly going to find a couple of bodies in good condition around here? Everybody I've come across is either dead, rotting, or already possessed by a spirit."

"You mentioned your mother. What is her state?"

"Mom is really bad sick and could go any minute." Simply saying the words caused my voice to quiver. I couldn't imagine a world without Mom—her hugs, her voice, her famous spaghetti, chili, and homemade lasagna.

"Yes, yes, such is the condition of every living person. Each one could go at any minute. Do you happen to know if she has life insurance?"

"You mean like money for me and Dad in case she dies?"

"No, no. The other kind where the One whose name shall not be mentioned gives her life after she passes? Surely if you were being baptized you know the name. But if you know, don't say it out loud. I have enough trouble with management as it is."

"I think Mom knows. In fact, Mom is why I'm here. I'm trying to buy her more time."

"Ah, a time traveler. Don't get many of those these days." He flipped a page, then another and paused, mumbling to himself. "Says here your father is not due to arrive for a good long while yet. His body might be an option. Perhaps we can adjust his date of arrival."

"I'm not giving up Dad. Does it say when Mom is due to arrive?"

"That's closely guarded information." He rocked back in his chair, giving me a somewhat sympathetic look. "I probably shouldn't mention this. Could get me in trouble big time. But I like your spunk and trunk, kid. I can see you have good bones. I can also tell you put family first, and that goes a long way with me. So here's what I'm going to offer you." Hail or something harder hit the window. "Hang on, that's Anna wanting to be let back in."

A torrent of ice fists pelted the pane so fast and hard I thought it might break the glass. With a snap of his fingers, the window opened. A disfigured mist seeped into the room and settled onto the pages of the open book on the floor.

"Should any book reviewers pass across my desk, I will be sure to let you know, Anna, I promise. Now back on the shelf."

With a shudder, the book flipped shut and, crawling crab-like up book spines, *Ferg* returned to its slot.

"If you're open to the idea of bringing your parents along," Sarge continued, "I'll give you our family package deal. Deliver you, your mom, and your dad, and I'll make sure you three get our best time-to-share-for-all-eternity unit. Top floor with a view of the Lake of Fire. The only reason I'm able to make this offer is that it's no trouble for me to process a married couple and a child at the same time. Family contracts are easier. Unless your parents are the sort who bicker. Are your parents the sort who bicker?"

"Not much. Mostly Mom gets on Dad about not vacuuming our apartment or dusting the floors often enough or loading and unloading the dishwasher, wiping out the bathroom sink, putting down the toilet seat, helping her unload the groceries, putting away the groceries, taking out the trash ... that sort of thing."

"With your father's accrued days left until his death and your mom's infinitesimally small amount remaining, I can sum the two figures as one. Except for a small processing fee, your debt would be paid in full. Of course, if you wish to add a gratuity, I would be most grateful."

"I'm not about to give up my parents. Why on earth would you even ask something like that?"

"First off, you are *under* the earth, not on it. And second, it's only a few hours your mom is losing. Three to be exact."

"Three? Are you sure? Mom seemed in pretty good shape when I waded out into the creek?"

"Oops. Sorry. Wasn't supposed to let that slip." He ran his finger down the page. "Cerebral aneurysm."

"But the cancer is in her lungs," I argued.

"And spread to her noggin," he replied. "Give her up now along with your father and your parents will be of some value to you. Wait until she expires and you will still need two bodies."

"But even if I do all this, won't I still be dead?"

"Well, you are the bright one, aren't you?"

On the desk, a pink conch shell vibrated.

"I need to answer this. Could be important. Probably not, but one can hope."

"Wait. Maybe I could give you someone else's body?" Here I was thinking of Mary Alice Davis. Not that I had any reason to wish Mary Alice dead. I didn't even know her.

Wait? What am I thinking? I don't even know this person. Stop it!

"There's a deal on the table, and time is running out." The hourglass on his desk was, in fact, running sand out of its top chamber. "You are not likely to get better terms than these. Around here things go from bad to worse, not the other way around."

The pink conch shell blared like a broken trumpet.

The little man picked up the shell. "Sergeant of Arms, Hands, and Fingers. How can I hurt you?"

Trying to keep my voice down, I asked, "How many bodies would it take to buy my mother more time?"

Covering the opening of the pink conch, he whispered, "Are you suggesting I change your mother's date of death?"

"No one has to know. Change a couple of numbers. The book is right in front of you."

"Accounting would notice right away. And then the big boss would realize I'm fudging the books."

From inside the conch shell, a voice started shouting.

"You like this job?" I asked.

"It's worse than my previous position, but in these parts the climb down the corporate ladder is inevitable." Sarge swiveled in his chair, turning his back to me. "Bradshaw? Ricky? Yes. As a matter of fact—he swiveled back toward me—I'm looking at him as we speak?" He mouthed to me, "Boss says he has a file on you."

Not surprised.

"But, sir, he hasn't been processed, disassembled, cataloged, and ... Right, sir. I understand, sir."

"Two bodies in good shape?" I asked.

Sarge nodded. "Very well, sir. I'll have him sent down for processing and punishing."

I had no idea where I'd come up with two bodies, but I had a rough outline of a plan. Not a great plan, but an okay plan. *It might work*, I thought. *It has to work. Mom's life depends on it. Maybe Becky's too.*

With Sarge staring at the back wall again, I bolted. Seeing no one in the hallway, I turned and—

From out of nowhere a fat fist hit my bony chin so hard it nearly knocked my skull from its spine. Crumpling to the floor, I rolled onto my side.

"Warned you I would chase you to hell and back." Barking Bart's odorous breath had not improved with his death. "So glad you could join me."

CHAPTER FOURTEEN

SETTLING OLD SCORES ON THE RACK

Barking Bart hoisted me onto my feet, then slammed me against a wall. "You want to know why I use the whip? The sword is too quick. With a jab to the chest, even a Whittle Shrimp like yourself would bleed out quick-like."

"But I'm down to bones."

"No matter. Protocol is protocol. The lash, now, can peel flesh one narrow strip at a time. Of course in your case, I'll be peeling your bones bit by bit."

Becky wandered past, filing her nails.

"I thought you were going to stay with your ship?"

"Boat. And it sank," she answered. "I heard there's a chance I can talk to someone about swapping my life for that of Mary Alice Davis. I like that option better than waiting for you to pull off one of your unbelievably dumb rescue plans."

"How do you know my plan would be dumb?"

"Seriously, Rog. If you want me to take you seriously, you need to stop with the lame jokes."

"What joke? I've gone to pirate land before, and I've always come back. Usually after making things better."

"Things don't look so good for you now, so I'll stick with my plan."

"You, with me," Barking Bart said, shoving me forward. "You need to see what happens to them who fail to give the Devil his due." Calling over his shoulder, he added, "You too, wench. The bigger the audience the harder the executioner works to inflict pain."

At the end of a long hallway, we passed through a series of doors and came to a large space illuminated by torches affixed to walls. Row after row of torture gadgetry stretched out before me, much of it similar in appearance to the sort of fitness equipment you might find in a workout gym. Victims in various states of decay pulled cables through pulleys and hoisted bars with barbs connected to the handles. Every apparatus appeared to be invented in order to inflict maximum agony. Words of discouragement handwritten in blood had been placed about the room.

At the Thumb Screw:

Your Pain, Our Gain.

Below a Dunking Machine positioned over a kettle of steaming hot water:

No Drain, More Pain.

Beneath Th e Knee Splitter:

No Strain, No Pain.

The Breaking Wheel appeared to be popular, as did the Flaying Platter:

No Pain, No Grease Stain.

The seat of the Flaying Platter was caked with crusty, fried skin. A workout coach with a whip and barbed club kept things lively by yelling, "I'm hell-bent on whipping you lowlifes into shape. Hop to it! Hop to it!"

The piece of equipment I found most interesting was the Rack, or rather the victim strapped onto The Rack. Tew Few lay face down on a wooden platform configured with a system of cranks. With each turn, the ropes tied to Tew Few's wrist bones and anklebones stretched.

"This room is for those who refuse to give up the ghost," Barking Bart said. "That be why we call it the Wait Room. We cannot harvest the remains until a body breathes its last." He gave The Rack's lever a half-turn, prompting Tew Few to let out a sickening howl.

"But he's only a skeleton," I protested.

"And still his death be worth savoring." Barking Bart pushed the lever another click. "Only reason he still be breathing be that I want to enjoy this as long as I can."

Another click and Tew Few screamed in a way that turned the stomach I did not have.

"Fellers and some lasses will sometimes hold out for hours, begging for mercy or a miracle. When none comes—help and salvation never come to those who suffer in this realm—they will give up loved ones. That be why all about this room, there be weeping and lashing of teeth."

"I think it's weeping and gnashing of teeth?" Becky said.

"You say gnashing, I say lashing, but which of us be without teeth now?"

"Becky, don't you care that he's mocking you?"

"People mocking me is nothing new, Rog. That's what sent me here, remember?"

I got what Barking Bart was saying, and I did not much like his insinuation. I could give up Mom and Dad, clear my debt, and be done with life and suffering. Or not.

"I admit your chum be not much to look at now, but except for that one missing appendage, his frame and chassis be in near-perfect condition. He will make a fine start on a rebuild. Till then ..." Barking Bart gave the lever another half-turn.

"Please stop," I said.

"Please? Now that be an odd word to speak in a place where no hearts, no mercy, and no hope be found."

Leading Becky and me down a short, darkened row, Barking Bart made us stop at a wide, bloodstained wooden bench. "This be the Boss's very own contraption. He came up with it during the Dark Ages when proselytizing was spreading at an alarming rate. Have a seat."

"Thanks, but I'll stand."

"I said *sit*." With a hard slap, he shoved me onto the wooden bench. "The Rat Rack be reserved for those who still espouse some cockamamie notion that there be a better life after their time on earth. After a go with a rat, a feller will soon give up some such silly nonsense."

Unable to shut out the screams of Tew Few—and with all my attention now fixed on a large wharf rat held by its tail—I turned away from the sight of my friend's suffering. Seated with my back to the other workout coaches, a pair of pirates approached from behind, grabbed my arms and legs, and wrapped me in cloth, mummy-like.

"A little heads up would have been nice."

"Heads up, heads down," Becky said. "I hardly think it would have mattered. From the looks of things, you're headed for a strenuous workout. You might as well get your mind right, Rog."

Lashing me to the wooden workout bench, the pair of pirates returned to torturing an old woman with a walker.

"Now, what I be about to do next, you will simply loathe. First, I will place this rat on your chest, like so."

Like the rats that had attacked us on the beach, this one showed fierce-looking fangs that glistened with saliva.

"Next, I will place this wooden bucket upside down on your chest, like so, and lash it down snug." With a rope, Barking Bart tied the bucket tight to my chest with the trapped rat under it.

"Finally, I will put newly harvested flesh around and over your body so as to arouse that varmint's appetite."

Due to the graphic nature of what came next, I'll avoid describing how Barking Bart filleted a naked corpse.

"Now then, once that rat tries to escape and finds it can't—and no doubt by now you can feel that critter starting to squirm about—it will start to claw its way through the cloth and into your chest. Trapped in your rib cage, the little feller will commence to gnawing on bones. It will only be a matter of time before you be begging for mercy. But like I mentioned, no mercy will come. Only way to stop the torment be for you to give up your Mum and Pop. Do that and I will move you onto less torturous equipment. Dumbbells be a good choice for you. With only an empty skull, I can commence a melody of ringing in your head that will feature almost any song you like long as it not be a hymn. Those be off limits in this realm."

"SAILS. TO QUARTERS! TO QUARTERS!"

In the hallway—and with a speed not normally seen in the walking-dead—the *Dutchman*'s pirates rushed to the ladder. Immediately, the Wait Room became crowded with crew charging past me, each armed to the teeth—or in the case of at least one pirate, a single tooth.

"Drat it all. I wanted to watch Whittle Shrimp squirm. You," he said to Becky, "keep an eye on him until I get back. He be a slippery one, so don't let him out of your sight. Savvy?"

"No way I'm taking responsibility for Rog."

"Can't help but notice you're skinny as a mizzen mast. Are you eating enough?"

Suddenly tearing up, Becky turned away, dabbing her eyes.

"I swear on me timbers, if Whittle Shrimp goes missing, there will be more barbs like that. You get my meaning?"

Sniffling, Becky nodded.

Turning toward the door, Barking Bart gave the Rack another half turn, producing an excruciatingly loud scream from Tew Few.

"Payback be hell, Whittle Shrimp. And the worst of your back pay be yet to come."

CHAPTER FIFTEEN

MERCILESS MARAUDERS AND HEARTLESS HORRORS

In the Wait Room, pirates walked about like zombies. Their twisted limbs with bones sticking out against stretched skin created odd-shaped lumps. Their joints creaked with every clumsy step. And when they lifted their arms, gross, saggy flesh flaked off, leaving behind this disgusting trail of rotting skin. As they dashed past, some gave Tew Few a hard punch. Others rapped the bucket hard in an attempt to excite the rat—though the rodent needed no additional motivation.

"Sorry, Rog. I had no idea."

Her words, subtly hinting at concern, filled me with a mixture of frustration and hope. "Sorry is as sorry does."

"Oh, so now you're quoting a headless person?"

"Hey, cut me some slack. It's me with a rat gnawing on my rib cage, not you."

Reverting to a tone of annoyance, Becky replied, "Whatever."

"No, really, loosen this rope."

"You heard what that gross-looking man with the whip said, the one wearing what I'm sure is an adult diaper. If you escape, it's me with a rat on my chest."

"You honestly believe that someone wielding a whip, barking orders at zombie pirates, and taking sadistic delight from the suffering of others isn't going to torture you too?"

"Well, I do now."

"Mate, I kin not take much more of this," Tew Few said, his voice strained and filled with weariness. "What be yer plan fer getting us out of this fix?"

Concerned that Tew Few might give up hope, I said, "Working on it." To be honest, I had no plan, not even a seed of a plan. All I had was a rat running loose in my rib cage.

"How's your cheek, Becky?"

"How do you think? It hurts."

Watching Tew Few writhe in pain, I asked him, "If I get you out of that contraption, you think you can walk?"

"N-not sure," he stammered, his voice weak. "I-I can't even sit up, mate, let alone walk."

"No worries. Once I get free, I'll go topside, find us a skiff to steal, and be back for you."

Summoning all the strength I could, I rocked the bench side-to-side until … *CRASH!*

On deck, Becky and I took cover under a longboat. Though moving with the rigidity of zombies, the pirates hurried to their stations. Still gripped in a violent, thrashing storm, I spied a white sail with a red cross at the edge of the blackness.

"Mercy ship!" one of the crew shouted. "No doubt one filled with invalids, lame, blind, crippled, mute, and many others afflicted with various deadly diseases. A fine catch indeed."

At the words *fine catch indeed* something within me snapped. To take advantage of the poor, the lame, the blind seemed heartless. Then again, they were pirates possessing bodies with dead hearts.

"Rog, you're rattling," Becky said. "Are you okay?"

"We have to do something," I whispered. *But what? There are too many.*

"Bend on sails, you sorry stiffs! Or you will have no racks to bend." Apparently, Barking Bart had sunk to the rank of ship's foreman aboard the *Flying Dutchman*. "Deckhands, prepare to lower the gigs! Gun crews to the ready!"

I needed to act fast. I tried to crawl out, but weak and breathless from where the rat had gnawed me, I could hardly lift the edge of the longboat. Like a trapped rat, I slunk back to avoid detection.

"Boarders to the longboats!" Barking Bart called. "Stand by to board!"

Two-by-two, "boarders" crawled over the starboard side and settled into longboats. Soon, they'd flip over our boat, exposing us.

"You, man, go aloft posthaste," barked Barking Bart. "On my command, set topgallants. Rest of you, grab a musket or pistol. We will rake that vessel from stem to stern."

Those not in the boarding party hurried to grab firearms. One level down, the rumble of cannon wheels rolled over wooden floors. Soon, gunners would be in a position to blast the hapless vessel.

From aloft a voice called, "She's but a league away, sir. Perhaps less. An easy mark she'll be."

This is it, I thought. These dead pirates are going to find us and do even worse things than before. On the side of my cheekbone, I felt hot tears rolling down. Becky had eased closer, kneeling right over the top of me. She silently sobbed.

"Boarders at the ready?"

From the crew in longboats, sabers rattled, and curses rang out.

"Ship of the sick and afflicted, indeed. She will receive no mercy this day."

As the pirates readied to blast the hospital ship, my thoughts raced to Mom and countless others confined to hospital beds or languishing at home, clinging to life. They remained oblivious to the impending horror that awaited them once they passed from life to death.

"What be our charge?" Barking Bart shouted to the crew.

"STEAL! KILL! DESTROY!"

"That's the spirit of torment, men. One musket shot per man and no more," said Barking Bart. "Let the sword do its deadly business. I want her crew to suffer and suffer long."

A whispering chant of "pain, pain, pain," went up from among the *Dutchman's* crew.

I whispered to Becky, "Still think you'll get a fair deal with this crew?"

At Barking Bart's command, the gun crew sent a shot across the hospital ship's bow. Her ship's pilot must have realized that an attempt to run would prove futile, for he swung into the wind, heaving to. In reply, the *Dutchman* crowded on all sails, reaching the ship within minutes and bringing the fierce storm of blackness with it. From beneath the longboat, I watched passengers in hospital gowns gather along their ship's railings. Hoisting mops and brooms, some prepared to defend themselves. Others too weak to stand leaned on walkers and canes, their fists raised in defiance.

"Luff sails," called Barking Bart. "Boarders over the side!"

The *Dutchman's* crew lowered longboats. With her small armada of marauders armed with muskets, pistols, cutlasses, and knives, the fleet of pirates rowed across, jeering and pronouncing deadly curses. Only when the lead longboat neared the hospital ship did her crew of invalids rise in force. The blast of a lone cannon took the boarding party completely by surprise.

The mops and brooms had obviously been a decoy—a ploy to lull the pirates into a false expectation of an easy fight. Instantly, the lame, crippled, and even the blind raised muskets and fired at the fleet. In a panic, some pirates dove into the water while others ducked for cover. Those in the second fleet of longboats got off a round. While the rest of the longboats pivoted into position to return fire, a second row of invalids rose from below the railing and fired point-blank into the first fleet, sinking all but one longboat.

Stunned and thrashing in the water as only a zombie pirate can, the pummeled crew swam back to the *Dutchman*. Fingers had been ripped away, arms mangled. Holes had punctured chests, legs, and in one case, a pirate's forehead. Though none bled, they did appear weakened by the attack.

Cheering their success, those aboard the mercy ship hurriedly reloaded their small arsenal, but if they expected Barking Bart to relent, they underestimated the viciousness of his black heart.

From the port side, out of sight, he oversaw the launch of a second wave of boarders. This fleet came on in greater numbers and to avoid directed fire, spread out. With shots picking off any aboard the hospital ship who dared to stand and fire, those in the second fleet of longboats soon reached their prize. Tossing up grappling hooks, they gained access and clambered aboard. Swift, deadly blows overwhelmed the defenders. Within moments, the rest of the boarding party swarmed aboard the hospital ship and cut down any who dared to fight back.

Aiming a pistol at the bearded face of a massively large pirate, a frail-looking man in a green hospital gown made a weak gesture of defense. With a roundhouse swing of his forearm, the marauder clubbed the patient across his face, sending the victim stumbling back. Helpless and bleeding from his nose and lip, the pirate grabbed the little man by his hair, lifted his head, and slid the cutlass blade across his throat. With the small man's body still quivering and his severed jugular veins spurting blood, the pirate rolled the victim's decapitated head across the deck as though it were a bowling ball.

Another pirate bent a man's arm behind his back and walked the captive to a lower spar, wrapped a rope around his neck, and winched him upward, hanging the victim from the foremast.

Three pirates chased a young woman to the front of the ship, blocking her moves each time she sought to evade them. Cornered, she swung fists only to be slapped and kicked in return. While one pirate held her from behind, another nailed her feet to the deck and her hands to the bowsprit.

The remaining crew were beaten into submission, blindfolded, and dragged in front of the ship's swivel cannon. One by one, each was forced to kneel before the end of the barrel.

I craned my neck and looked up at Becky. "Seen enough?"

Dabbing her eyes, she nodded. With so many of the *Dutchman's* crew celebrating, cheering, and preparing to ferry more crew over to the mercy ship, none seemed to notice that Becky slipped and crawled toward a deck hatch.

One level down in an empty hallway, out of earshot of any who might stumble past, I asked, "If I try to escape, will you tell?"

"I've kept my end of the bargain. I gave you up. Now please, get me off this ship."

"Run back to the torture room, but be careful. I can't have you get caught. Free our friend. I'll be along in a moment."

"What are you going to do?"

"Buy us more time."

I tested the knob of the door leading into the office of the Sergeant of Arms. When the knob turned and the door creaked open, I paused, listened, and peered in. With Sarge's chair pushed back, the room stood empty.

I slipped in, flipped pages in the Book of Life, found the names of my parents and with a quill, altered their death dates. There came a thumping on the deck above. Making a few more notations, I quickly put the quill back in its inkwell. When the clomping of feet in the hallway faded, I peered out and hurried to the Wait Room.

"We can't go back the way we came," I said to Becky and Tew Few. "We'll have to find another exit." I nodded toward a door marked BRIG. "I have an idea."

Captives sat confined behind bars, some screaming to be set free, others whimpering. Dimly flickering torches offered scant light. I found a skeleton key hanging on a peg and unlocked each cell door.

"You two, hide in that mop closet."

"Hide where?" Becky asked.

I pointed at the sign that said SWAB ROOM at the end of the brig.

"Hurry, Rog. This place reeks."

I unlocked door after door but not a soul stepped out. Though screaming to be set free, none dared take a chance at stepping out into the light.

Joining the others, I pointed up to the beams. "These support joists probably reach up to the rudder post. They help reinforce the ship's stern." I turned to Tew Few. "Can you pull yourself up?"

"Sorry, mate. I be plum tuckered out."

"Give him a hand up."

"Is that supposed to be funny?" Becky asked.

"Not this time. Near the top of the rudder post, there should be a small access door leading out. Most ship carpenters leave a way to access the interior of the rudder post for repairs. You may have to kick through and bust a hole."

"What are you going to be doing while I'm doing whatever it is you asked me to do?"

"Trying to convince these prisoners to escape while they still can."

CHAPTER SIXTEEN

HELD CAPTIVE
BY OUR CONVICTIONS

Sitting in a dimly lit cell, staring at the floor, one prisoner appeared lost in thought.

Standing outside the cell, holding open the door, I said, "Hey, you're free to go. You can get out of here, escape this place. Let's go."

The man looked up, eyes filled with weariness. "Escape? Is that what you believe I require? Kindly attend to your own affairs, young man."

"I have the keys. I'm setting you free. You can't seriously want to stay locked up on this ship."

He paused, as though reflecting on my suggestion. "Indeed, it is undeniable that my existence within these confines has been far from ideal and rife with injustice. I have endured immense suffering at the hands of others ... been deceived, robbed, and betrayed by those I loved most."

The foul stench of human excrement left me nauseous. Inside cramped cells without so much as straw for bedding, water rushed up from the bilge and over the feet of the prisoners.

"There you go. This is your chance to break free, to start over."

"Young man, my departure from this place shall not rectify matters. Granted, I have my faults, yet my transgressions do not warrant the conditions in which I now find myself."

"Right. That's my point. We all make mistakes and deserve punishment, but there's another option. And it's not on this ship."

"Were I to do so, I would be violating my convictions. I possess an unwavering adherence to my belief that I shall soon see justice. And when those who wronged me appear before me, I shall give them an earful."

Amidst the echoes of captives' screams, I couldn't help but wonder, *Why would anyone in their right mind choose to stay?* "Trust me, if you think you or anyone else is going to get justice on this ship, you're being naïve."

"You speak like one of those sanctimonious religious zealots who rail on the corner of Richmond and Dundas. Their incessant proclamations that we are all sinners in need of redemption rile me to no end. Mere poppycock, I assure you."

"But don't you want relief from your pain and suffering?"

From the far end of the brig, two pirates stepped into the torchlight's dim glow. "Damon, check the swab closet. If I know that Whittle Shrimp, he'll be hiding in there like the rat he be."

At Barking Bart's mention of *a swab closet*, I got a sickening feeling in the space where my stomach should have been.

"Me, sir? You know how fearful I be of tiny spaces with cleanin' supplies."

SMACK! "Swab closet, Damon, and be quick about it."

"While I have committed transgressions," the prisoner continued, "I firmly believe that, at my core, I am a virtuous man. I have extended aid to the destitute and upheld obligations to my family. Perchance my stance is rooted in idealism, but by remaining here, I retain the opportunity to bear witness to the perpetrators and watch them face their just comeuppance."

Backing away, I whispered, "You know things are not going to magically improve in here, right?"

Wearing a maroon turban, black robe, and scarlet sash, the lead pirate worked his way down the brig, slamming doors shut as he passed.

"Nor shall those who subjected me to such cruelty escape the retribution they so deserve. Rather than escape, I prefer to endure endless torment in order to watch my enemies receive the lash, leg irons, and torture due them."

There it was; the man needed to see justice done to others but not himself. Forgiveness meant letting his enemies off the hook, and that would leave him vulnerable and appearing weak. I suppose holding on to his grievances had become part of his identity, a way to find comfort and validation in his prison. Remaining in misery gave him a sense of control and empowerment.

"You dwelling on how others have hurt you might give you a sense of control, I get that. But this opportunity to escape will only remain open a few moments longer."

THUMP! CRACK! SNAP!

From inside the swab closet, it sounded as though Becky had taken a sledgehammer to the rudder shaft.

"Swab closet, you idiot pirate!"

Staggering side to side with the stumbling agility of a fresh corpse in need of a serious caffeine fix, the zombie swashbuckler crept toward me.

"Hey, Rog, we busted out a hole. But it's really a long way down, and the waves are huge."

The door suddenly swung open. An immense pirate scowled at me, blocking my escape. In a blur of steel, the pirate sliced the air with a huge, curved saber.

"You coming?"

Trapped and with only a mop for defense, I kicked the bucket, nailing the pirate in the face. Shaking his head as though dazed, he gave me a look that could kill—and perhaps he might have if Becky hadn't sent broken boards and other debris falling on him.

"Last call, Rog. I'm about to jump."

Tumbling out of range of the blade's deadly stabbing, I yelled up, "Want to know a secret?"

"Not really," Becky answered.

"Fine, I'll keep it to myself." Grabbing the smelly mop, I defended myself. "En garde, you filthy pirate." I'll admit, it sounded better in my empty head.

With a sudden thrust, his cutlass jabbed at my rib cage, passing between two bones and missing my spine.

"Okay, Rog, what's the big secret?"

The pirate pulled back his cutlass and slashed at my neck. Had I not ducked, he'd have left me looking like Snake, only with less skin.

"I never said it was a big secret."

"Small secret, whatever."

Quickly, I jabbed the pirate's face with a clump of smelly mop hairs, knocking off dried skin. The blow sent him momentarily stumbling back out the door.

"If forced to pick between big and small, I'd definitely say my secret was on the large size."

"Seriously, Rog, sometimes having a conversation with you is exhausting."

"I changed your death date," I yelled up. "That's my big secret."

"You fight like my little sisters," growled the pirate.

"I would think after having offspring as ugly as you, your parents wouldn't chance to have more kids."

My taunting prompted the pirate to use a quick double-slash that brought his cutlass down on my shoulder bone. Swinging the mop, the two of us fenced and jousted the way children will do at a pirate party.

"You're not going to die, Becky. At least not for a very long time."

Something almost like a smile spread all of a half inch across the pirate's face. "But *you* die today." With several vicious swipes, the pirate again attempted to separate my skull from neck bones—and would have if I hadn't blocked his blows with the mop handle. My perfectly executed defense left me holding something like a nunchuck with frayed hair.

"Is that all you've got? Really?" I asked. "I expected more from you."

Smirking, he replied, "I'll feed you to the sharks."

"Oh, yeah? We'll see who mops up who."

I never got the chance to deliver the fatal blow. *SNAP!* The tip of a whip popped the side of my skull.

"No point in fighting back, Whittle Shrimp. I know about your whittle trick."

"Trick?"

Another snap popped my kneecap.

"About how you changed your Mum's death date."

Moving first into a sitting position, I then balanced on my knees, stood, and reached for the next beam above.

"I changed it back. Dead your mum be." Barking Bart flicked his wrist, flogging my anklebones.

"You're lying."

"And dead you'll be when I be done with you."

"There's a rowboat below us, Rog. I'm going for it!"

Barking Bart cracked his whip, its end wrapping around the rafter on which I stood.

"Wait, Becky! I'm almost there!"

"Join our crew, Whittle Shrimp, and I'll give you a low position with opportunities for demotions."

Standing on tiptoes, I grabbed the next rafter. "I'd rather die than serve aboard a ship with a crew led by you."

"Was hoping you would say that." Barking Bart growled. "Saves me the trouble training you how to kill with skill."

"I'm jumping, Rog. See you if I see you."

Barking Bart pulled a dirk from under his loincloth. With a flip of his wrist, he sent the small dagger flying into the middle of my chest. *THUD!* The dirk stuck in the wall behind me.

"Ha! You missed."

"But I won't miss," moaned the other pirate. Drawing a flintlock pistol from his waist sash, Damon the pirate aimed and pulled the trigger. The shot went wide.

"Ha! You missed too." I scampered up onto the next rafter.

Damon whipped out a second pistol, aimed, and ... missed again.

"The two of you have terrible aim."

YANK! TUG! CRASH!

I hit the bottom of the mop closet, my bones scattering across the floor.

Barking Bart stood over me. "Did you know that after the spirit leaves your body, the soul keeps living for, well ... all eternity? Now, I thrive on making others suffer and watching them squirm in agony. For me, your soul be but to toy with, a plaything you might say. So first, I'll torture you endlessly, breaking you down bone-by-bone until there be nothing left. And then, I'll do it all over again, forever and ever. And you want to know why, Whittle Shrimp?"

Terrified, I shook my skull.

"Cause when I gave you a choice to join our crew you said 'never.' And now never will be how long before you get relief from the pain of what's to come. Damon, get him in a transport. Time we deliver Whittle Shrimp into the Cave of Knaves on The Isle of Abaddon."

CHAPTER SEVENTEEN

THE ISLE OF ABADDON: GATEWAY TO TORMENT

Before us lay a maze of channels, each leading off into blackness. With only a lantern hanging off the longboat's bow to illuminate our course, we glided into a meandering creek that gradually led us under low branches. Only the squawking and hooting of swamp creatures and the gentle slapping of water against the boat's sides disturbed the silence.

Tucking Tew Few's coat tightly around him, I said, "Sorry you didn't make it off safely. I gave Becky strict orders to take care of you."

"No worries, mate. It whar my choice. I feared the jump would break me inter tiny pieces."

Behind us, the faint outline of the *Dutchman* glowed orange with flames amidst its ever-present dark storm. A dense, steamy mist hung over the swamp, its air heavy and oppressive and filled with the stench of rot and decaying flesh.

With Becky and Tew Few casting looks at me suggesting *THIS IS BAD!* I tried my best to come up with a plan of escape, but nothing came to mind. Then again, when you have no mind, it's hard to form a plan.

"Thar ne'er whar any chance, mate. Thar ne'er whar."

"But before, you told me as long as someone loved us, we still had a chance."

"Fer fellers like you and me, life be but random chances that end up leading us ter a watery grave."

"But she didn't ask for this." I stroked Becky's hair with a boney finger.

She replied with more sniffling. I hugged her tighter.

"Yer missy fell in with the wrong crowd. It happens."

The fact that Becky didn't reply or complain about him using the word *missy* left me concerned that she'd given up hope as well.

Next to me, a phantom figure piloted the longboat, his face concealed by a hooded shroud. Or perhaps there was no face to see, for since he first stepped aboard, I had not detected the slightest hint that the longboat's pilot was anything more than a ghoulish specter meant to ferry me to a place of torment. A sickle, held in place by a narrow strap, rested across his back. Had Barking Bart told me our ferryman was the Grim Reaper I would have believed it.

"There it be, The Isle of Abaddon and the end of all who perish without any hope. In case you missed my point"—Barking Bart jabbed my cheekbone with a dirk—"that be you and your puny crew, Whittle Shrimp."

Barking Bart announced this with such delight that I felt sure he'd waited for this moment since the instant the Kraken tossed him into the sea.

Far ahead, towering above the swamp's jungle canopy, an enormous volcano spewed molten lava into the air. Its thundering eruption painted the black sky with orangish-red streaks, adding a hint of illumination for our passage into the swamp.

"Eternal death and confinement in Hades await every soul whose deeds be judged as wicked. That also be you and your puny crew, Whittle Shrimp."

Gulls—down to bones, like me—screeched overhead, their claws dropping seashells on us.

"Plan?" Becky whispered.

"No jawing while rowing," said Barking Bart.

"But I'm not the one rowing," Becky replied.

"What's with you and grub? You getting enough chow? Why, you be scrawny as a bird. What do you say, Whittle Shrimp? Don't you think the lass ought to add some meat to her bones?"

Suddenly breaking into tears, Becky pressed herself against me. With my jawbone crushed and skull cracked due to the beating I'd received upon my capture, pulling Becky into my arms took great effort. Still, I tried. From the looks of things, I would not have many more opportunities to comfort the girl I had a crush on.

Thump! Bump! Leaning over the edge of the boat, I spied a massive tentacle snaking across the water behind us, its flared suckers floating just below the surface.

"Best make speed," Barking Bart instructed. "This swamp be guarded by mischievous creatures of a large, heavily-armed sort."

With fierce determination, the ferryman frantically worked his rudder paddle. To my horror, the creatures circled us, tentacles threatening to pull us over in anticipation of a tasty meal.

Reaching into a sack he had packed for our trip, Barking Bart retrieved the lower half of a human arm and, with a quick flip of his wrist, sent the appendage flying. At its loud *splash*, the water churned with octopuses rushing toward the meaty treat.

"They'll be back soon," he said to the pilot. "Best shake a leg or it'll be our leg they be shaking." Shifting his gaze toward Becky. "Speaking of legs ..." He reached for Becky's knee.

I slapped his hand away.

"Insolent and rebellious to the end," he said. "I have a remedy for that."

Smack! Whack! Jab!

"Sticks and stones may break my bones, but—"

Stab! Whap! Thwack!

The first few blows landed against my skull, the remainder on tentacles creeping over the transom. Acting quickly, the ferryman joined the fight and swung his sickle with a fierce slash that struck an octopus with the face of a man square across its eyes. Apart from the creature's immense size, the squid's bulbous head bore a striking resemblance to my own face.

A second slash sent the squid sinking back into the depths of the swamp, but by that point, the glow of the longboat's lantern had begun to illuminate a sign hanging from a lifeless tree stump.

Welcome to the Isle of Abandon: Please Excuse Our Destruction

"They misspelled the name of this place," I muttered.

"Right you be to point out that mistake, Whittle Shrimp, for here every fault, every error be identified, magnified, and its spokesman crucified. Inside that volcano is a god-forsaken cavern filled with molten lava where the most twisted and malevolent demons that ever crawled out of the darkest corners of hell be waiting to have their way with you. Ferryman, do you have a preferred port of entry?"

Our ghoulish pilot looked up, a bony finger pointing at hand-painted arrows. In the bow lantern's passing spray of light, I took in the miserable destinations that awaited us.

Straight to Hell—direct route
(steep decline, strenuous walk, not for the faint of heart)

Sure as Hell—wide path, paved with good intentions
(broad, slow-descending, easy walk, often crowded)

Hell of a Mess—a maze with interlocking trail
(map and compass recommended)

All Hell Breaks Loose
(*treacherous, watch for falling rocks,
ideal for those who seek adventure*)

Gates of Hell
(*main entrance to Cave of Knave, docks often full,
wait times can last an eternity*)

Hell and Back—a circular loop
(*ideal for those who like to procrastinate and
put off the inevitable*)

Snowball's Chance—seasonal
refreshment stand at the entrance
(*closed due to global warming*)

Cold Day in Hell—ice baths
(*perfect after a hot day at sea, also closed due to global warming*)

Living Hell—grueling walk
(*ideal for those who refuse to give up the ghost*)

"Here, your choices of torture be endless, Shrimp, and your misery never-ending. Here, it be our joy to crush your soul with impunity."

Before I could respond with some snide comment and lie about how I wasn't afraid, a serpent dropped from a low-hanging branch and landed in Becky's lap. Screaming, she tried scooting away.

Barking Bart, showing no fear of the snake, bent close toward its diamond-shaped head. "Say again, Boss?" Flicking its tongue at the air, the serpent hissed louder. "Boss wants us to pass through Gates of Hell. Says there be some paperwork that needs updating before these three can enter the Cave of Knaves."

With several hard tugs on the rudder paddle, the pilot veered the longboat into an even narrower canal, one blocked by silken webs stretching from bank to bank. Hairy wolf spiders as big as my hand jumped on us.

In a blur, the serpent's fangs sank into Becky's tender flesh, prompting a shriek that echoed off the swamp's canopy rooftop. Its deadly work done, the snake's sinuous form glided away. Clutching her neck, Becky collapsed, her body succumbing to the serpent's deadly poison.

"Becky? BECKY!"

"Here, mate, take my frock," Tew Few said. "Yer missy needs it more'n me now. I be done fer."

"Don't say that."

"It's true. Time ter give up the ghost." Tew Few's efforts to roll onto his back revealed the reality of his impending death. Clasping his hands over his ribcage, he sighed. "I could ne'er 'ave asked fer a better chum ter be by my side. Yer good crew, Ricky Bradshaw. Best I ever sailed with."

"You'll feel better once we get off this boat and onshore," I replied. "I'm sure of it."

"Whittle Shrimp, you speak foolishness," Barking Bart said. "Remember what I told you earlier? Things go from bad to worse?"

"Stood by me ter the end, you did, mate. Fer that I be eternally grate … grate …"

The sockets of Tew Few's empty eyes filled with a glimmer of light. Blood vessels instantly sprouted on his bony feet. Like thousands of new vines growing with enormous speed, each vein bloomed bright red, wrapping itself around bone. In the dim glow of the ferryman's lantern, Tew Few's skeletal frame transformed into that of a man with organs and muscles and tendons and sinew spreading across bones.

"Please don't go," I pleaded.

Just below his right wrist, the hook fell away, and a hand grew. His face formed last, flush with rosy cheeks, hinting at what he might have looked like as a younger man. With a momentary smile, Tew Few's half-grin went slack, and the corners of his mouth sagged. With a great sigh, the pupils of his eyes became fixed in a blank, upward stare.

"Sentimental slobs like Whittle Shrimp sicken me. Speaking of being sick ..." Nudging the ferryman, Barking Bart said, "Best push on faster. Our cargo looks to be perishing. I dare say this pair of love birds be down to their last breath."

At this disturbing pronouncement, I stared down at my limbs and watched in horror as blood vessels sprouted across the bones of my feet. Like my sailing buddy, life suddenly surged within. Which could only mean one thing.

I was dying—and this time for real.

CHAPTER EIGHTEEN

IN THE FACE OF ETERNAL DEATH, I FACE A HEARTBREAKING FAREWELL

Everything went crazy, bone-crunching painful in an instant. Intense, unbearable burning stabs wracked my reforming body. A tangled mess of nerves and blood vessels continued to wrap around bones, sending bolts of fire through every new nerve, creating a sensation of unbearable pain. With a convulsing scream, I arched my back, desperate for relief. Becky pressed against me and sobbed, her tears blending with gasps. Any other time I would have cozied up and consoled Becky, but with my body now completely back to normal, my brain was laser-focused on my own miserable agony.

Barking Bart grabbed a clump of my hair and yanked me up. "We have reached port, Whittle Shrimp. Time to give the Devil his due." His meaty arm slammed me against the transom, forcing me into a sitting position.

Before us, bracketed by steep rock walls on three sides, a large horseshoe-shaped cove bubbled with heat from molten lava streaming down. Skiffs and longboats and gigs of all types shuttled souls into the gaping mouth of a cave. Inside, something like an enormous furnace blazed.

"Hey, you dirty devils, over here. Take this pair into the Cave of Knaves for processing, but keep a firm grasp on this sorry lad. He already nearly escaped once."

Ghost-like spirits emerged from amidst plumes of smoke, their twisted forms dancing with glee. Encircling the longboat, these ghoulish spirits with fangs salivated at the sight of two fully formed bodies ready for harvesting.

Becky lifted her gaze to me. "I'm … c-cold."

Despite the pain caused by lifting my arms and using muscles to move, I hugged her tighter.

"I got you. I won't let go, promise."

In a gurgling gasp, she mustered, "Us? A couple?" Her words faltered, tender pauses lingering between each inhalation. With eyes falling shut, she nodded.

"Soul-catchers be coming for you two. Best prepare to meet your baker." At the word *baker*, Barking Bart chuckled a little, spoiling the tender moment Becky and I shared.

"Hang on," I whispered to Becky, "we'll find a way to make it out of this."

She fixed her gaze on mine as though searching for hope. But we both knew the truth. There would be no rest, no eternal peace. We'd seen the terror of the darkness.

She slumped against my chest. "You working on another of your great plans?"

"Blasted demons, they be so busy harvesting bodies my little cargo is of no account." Barking Bart pointed a fat finger at the faceless phantom piloting the longboat. "Keep an eye on these two. They try to jump ship, use that sickle."

Our pilot appeared to nod, though it may have been a breeze lifting the edge of his hood.

Stepping from the boat, Barking Bart approached the horde of ghastly ghouls by walking on octopus heads as if they were stones. I soon lost sight of him amidst the dark figures devouring the bodies of those destined for eternal destruction.

With eyes closed, Becky wheezed. "Kiss me." Her breathing became more erratic, punctuated by a rattling gasp each time she gulped air. "Like on the playground."

"Now? Right here?"

Her hand found the back of my head and attempted to pull her face close to mine, but she lacked the strength. Bending close, my lips found hers.

Our noses still touching, she purred. "Not bad."

"Better than Ed?"

In a croaking whisper, her breath warming my face, she said, "He slobbers." Then she tucked her head under my chin. "I don't know about you, but when I get back home I'm going to warn anyone who asks that ending your life the way I did is a terrible idea."

I snickered a little. "Or any other way."

She shifted her face so her breath warmed the side of my throat. When her exhalations stopped, I thought I'd lost her, but then she gasped, sending her into a coughing spasm. When the convulsions ceased, she said, "I like you, Ricky."

The warmth of her closeness, even in the insufferable heat, was easily the best thing I'd ever experienced.

"A lot. I have since kindergarten."

"But you call me Rog and make fun of me."

"Love hurts."

Love. There, she said it. Becky Nance loves me!

"So, what's your plan here … Ricky?"

She had begun to rally, her words coming easier, her breathing improved. I might have been encouraged except that I knew better from reading up on what to expect from Mom. Those few moments before death, a person will sometimes get a burst of energy. Becky now experienced such a rebound.

"I'm thinking we push the Grim Reaper into the water and paddle back to where we can …"

She lifted her face toward mine and, giving me a bittersweet smile, her lips briefly brushed against mine. "Umm, maybe with you, less talking?"

Knowing what was to come, Becky's kiss reminded me of how little time together we had left. I hugged her tighter, silently vowing not to mention any more crazy escape plans. "When we get back," I said, "I'm going to ask you out. Would that be okay?"

Her teeth chattering, Becky stuttered, "I … I'm … fre … freezing."

I knew why. I'd studied the family palliative care guide over and over until I knew it by heart. In the realm of the living, her heart was giving out. Unable to push enough blood to her extremities, her body slowly shut down. I hugged her so tight my new muscles ached. Her jaw went slack and by small degrees, her head rolled away from me as if she slept peacefully.

But she was not asleep. Her family had simply given up hope and pulled the plug. Which meant Barking Bart's declaration that he'd changed Becky's death date—and Mom's—was true.

With the ferocity of a pack of pit bulls, ghoulish demons rushed toward us. As with the other bodies ferried toward the massive cave of fire, the horde intended to devour Becky's body, but I would have none of it. Still clutching her, I shot to my feet, fell backward over the transom, and took us down into scalding, hot darkness.

CHAPTER NINETEEN

SURVIVAL OF THE FITNESS

There are dreams we recall, memories of moments never lived that we cannot erase from our minds.

Sometimes in the dead of night, we may come awake from a nightmare, our heart racing. For a few terrified moments, we fear that what we witnessed was real. Other times, we find ourselves pulled from our slumber with visions of people we have not seen for a very long time. Sometimes those people have died and passed on. Their appearance in our dreams might reassure us they are well, and that death has been kind to them. We may even awaken believing that we too will find peace in the grave.

Back last July on one of those global warming days that sets records, my family and I were melting at a city park in Virginia Beach, enjoying a skateboarding event. This guy who resembled an overzealous sports commentator wearing a pirate outfit and carrying a worn Bible marches right up to my dad and screams in his face. "Anyone who listens to the words of the Teacher will never see death. Do you believe this?"

Naturally, Dad was like, "Come on, Rick. Let's check out the half-pipe competition."

As we were walking away, Mom said to the man, "Tell me more."

That's Mom, always confronting confrontation with more engagement. Like, if Mom were a professional boxer, she would lean into her opponent and pound away at his ribs until he begged the ref to stop the fight.

"Not *a* teacher," the preacher yelled. "*THE* Teacher."

But I had already tuned out Mom and the preacher because Tony Hawk was doing insane flips and not even holding on to his board while doing it. Or at least someone who looked like Tony Hawk was flipping his board—which these days could be a lot of girls and guys.

Now, clinging to the girl I had a crush on and not feeling all that great, not even in my newly reformed and impressively fit body, the only thing I could focus on were the words of that lunatic pirate preacher: "You will never see death."

This was the guy who had convinced Mom she could kick cancer's butt. This was also the guy who promised if she had faith in the Teacher she'd be healed. Dad was so convinced the guy was a fraud that he had bet Mom twenty bucks this freak pirate would charge massively for his "hands of healing" prayer. My father lost big time. The pirate preacher charged nothing for his prayer or to place his hands on Mom.

No way this is going to work. That's what I thought while standing at the edge of the creek watching Mom smothered under the arms of the preacher, his wife, and a few other faithful followers—some of whom had all their teeth.

The thing was, *I had seen death*, and a lot of it—Becky and Tew Few, plus all those who'd been tortured to death on the mercy ship—so I did not feel all warm and fuzzy about what came next. And what came next had the appearance of a school prom, only worse.

Settling into a thick, gooey muck that left my feet stuck and burning in something like lava, I detected the steady beat of drums and riveting chords of electric guitars. A singer sang words that, though nonsensical, left Becky and me laughing. Behind her, Mom's mother led a conga line of dancers, all bent forward at the waist and twisting their hips with enthusiasm. Grandma looked as she had when she'd passed—short, pudgy, her face plump and beat red. The scowl Grandma had worn so often during her last years had been replaced by a broad smile. Small, blue eyes twinkled with laughter.

Others arrived on the dance floor—Grandpapa in a white, crew-neck tee shirt with a pack of cigarettes tucked in the hem of the shirt's short sleeve. My cousin, long dead, wandered onto the stage with her infant, the child she'd kept a secret from everyone but her mother. Uncle Jack, Dad's younger brother who'd been flattened while riding his Suzuki, waved to me.

They were all there watching Becky and me trying to dance with our feet stuck in the muck. Becky wore a white dress, its veil floating up and over her head. Except now her head was only a skull. I had shed my black tux coat but still wore the suit's cummerbund over a white shirt. It was like everyone we knew had turned out for our wedding reception. Only then did I begin to recognize the nonsensical tune "Celebration" by Kool and the Gang.

But there was nothing to celebrate or anything cool about what I felt. There was nothing but pain and the horror of watching Becky's flesh flake off and float away. When a dream is too real and goes on for too long, our mind begins to process the event. Logic kicks in, and we ask questions that crack the foundations of the dream.

That is what happened. The reality that I was drowning in blistering hot water yanked me wide awake. The enormous tentacle of a giant squid snaked its way around my quivering legs, tightening its grip with an unyielding force. With each passing moment, it pulled me downward, plunging me into a swirling abyss of scorching, lava-like sludge. The searing heat burned with the stings of a thousand Portuguese man o' war, leaving me at the mercy of the monstrous creature's grip.

Trapped, unable to escape, I ingested scalding hot water. The rancid, putrid odor of rotting flesh filled my nostrils. With each gulp, the horrifying truth became more real.

I was dying.

Out of air, arms flailing, I sank into a noxious, infernal liquid.

CHAPTER TWENTY

In total stillness, a wave of serenity washed over me, its cleansing tide lifting me beyond the boundaries of consciousness. Emerging from the water, my soul, weightless and suddenly unburdened by pain, left its mortal shell, soaring high above the longboat and the horror of souls streaming into the Cave of Knaves and toward a heavenly realm untethered to earth.

No longer constrained by my earthly body, I floated with the weight of a feather. My awareness of self and surroundings and knowledge of the afterlife swelled, filling me with peace.

Above, a radiant tunnel of light beckoned me, its kaleidoscope of colors pulling me upward into its brilliance. Only as an afterthought did I glance back.

There, far below, lay my body floating face up, eyes open wide, but I felt no fear, no shock. The weight of worry and dread, of terror and regrets dissolved. Only a blissful state of oneness with my surroundings swelled within me. In a moment of stunning clarity, I wondered why I had ever feared dying.

With my soul skipping across celestial stars, I reveled in blissful liberation.

Then, with the force of Black Bart's whip snatching me backward, an unseen power seized my soul. With a swift, violent tug, I was wrenched back into the grip of Davy Jones' watery grave, its merciless jolt shattering my transcendent euphoria. I had almost escaped the dangerous world of shipwrecks and ghostly crew and the mysterious presence of Davy Jones' Locker.

Jonah's spirit served as a warning to all who go down to the sea and I suppose to lubbers who make no provision for their passage out of the land of the living.

Disoriented, no longer burning hot but still submerged in lukewarm water, I clawed my way back into the realm of flesh and bone and broke the surface, coming up out of the creek gasping for air.

"Atta boy, me hearty! Buried with him in death, raised to walk in newness of life."

I blinked away water. *Buried in death?*

"Now that ye 'ave emerged from the depths of baptismal waters, I declare ye cleansed and reborn. Before ya lays a whole new soul ready to set sail upon the seas of faith. May yer compass always point true to the Almighty's guidance, and may ye chart a course in this life that be true."

Snorting, gulping air, I studied the pirate preacher. His wife, Mom, and the small crowd of faithful followers pressed in around me. A bunch of people were slapping me on the back as if I'd just won the Masters.

"Oh, Ricky, you're saved!" Mom squeezed me so tight I had flashbacks of the Kraken.

"How long was I … under?"

"A quick dip is all. Barely had time to pray over ya for you popped back up. Why, I've seen wine corks stay under longer."

I wheeled and grabbed Mom by the shoulders. "We have to get you to the hospital and fast."

"Why? I feel fine. I feel better than fine. Best I've felt in weeks."

Grabbing her hand, I tugged her up the short slope of the beach toward the sidewalk and space where we'd parked. "Trust me, Mom. We need to hurry. You don't have much time."

Mom's face scrunched up with a look of confusion. "Did you see something?"

"A lot of somethings. None of it good. And you're on borrowed time."

Captain's Log

On a cool November morning, the final day of our yacht charter arrived. Dad and I steered our small inflatable dinghy toward the south shore of Cape Lookout Bight. The wind had remained consistent from the northwest throughout the week, enabling us to sail smoothly from Beaufort to Wrightsville Beach and back, with a beam reach in both directions. Dad had graciously let me take charge as the captain for both legs of the journey. My counselor had suggested this voyage to give me some space between the events that took place in the creek weeks earlier.

Dad tilted the outboard, moving the prop clear of sand, and locked it in place. "You're not still dwelling on what happened with your mother, are you?"

With a firm grip on the inflatable's bow handle, I pulled the small rubber boat clear of the high tide line. "Only every minute."

"These things take time, Son, but it will pass. It always does."

"But it was different this time. More real than before, and more terrifying."

"I did a little reading up on what you went through. There is something called a baptism out-of-body experience. Though rare, sometimes people who get baptized will actually believe they have died."

"Are you saying what I witnessed didn't happen?"

"No, Son. I would never diminish what you went through or are feeling. It's just with your condition, we know that submersion in water is a trigger." Dad padlocked the motor to the outboard, then grabbed our rain jackets. "Even if an episode only lasts a few seconds, that might be enough to cause what you saw and experienced to take place."

Thunder boomed. From the south, low, roiling black clouds over the ocean swallowed more blue sky, turning the brilliance of dawn's light into a vivid veil of darkness and light.

Dad handed me my slicker, then slipped on his rain jacket. "Are the nightmares better or worse?"

"About the same. Last night I dreamed I was in prison, but it wasn't prison like we know. I was free to leave, but I had to be back by five. Otherwise, they'd come find me and put me in solitary. I went to a sports bar to watch a golf match on TV. A van pulled up and asked if I wanted to go surfing, so I hopped in. They parked on the side of a two-lane road and on soft, white sand, we hiked through trees and came out at the water. The waves and ocean looked just like this. I couldn't wait to get in the water, but something kept holding me back. When I looked down, I found irons like I'd seen in the brig, around my ankle. A chain snaked back into the woods. I knew the guards at the prison would pull me back if I tried to paddle out, that I'd never be free of the prison."

With the approaching storm, the wind died to dead calm. Dad and I dropped down on a low dune and looked southeast across the water. Sand fleas gnawed on my scalp and skin.

Dad asked, "Still thinking about dropping out after the fall semester?"

The first large, fat drops splatted on the sand by my feet. I glanced over my shoulder at Soul Survivor. Our chartered sailboat floated in the wide anchorage, its dark blue sail cover forming a break in the diamond pattern on the lighthouse. On flat, calm water, the hull shimmered white, reflecting the boat's profile.

"It's not like I won't be getting an education, Dad. Remote learning is only going to get better, and with study groups popping up online, it's not like I'll be a hermit. What

I experienced made me realize that sitting in a high school classroom with a bunch of kids only focused on grades, college, and careers that leave them bored is a waste of time."

"What about your friend Becky? Have you spoken to her since you visited her at the hospital?"

"We text some. She's better. Becky and Ed aren't together anymore. He and a girl named Mary Alice Davis were seen last week in the food court at the mall. I think if I asked Becky out she'd say yes, but I want to give her space. Like me, she's thinking of taking some time off from school. Her parents mentioned the family selling their home, buying an RV, and visiting all the national parks. If she does, maybe Becky and I could be part of our own study group."

Mom waved from the cockpit of the rented sailboat.

"Breakfast looks to be ready," Dad said. "Head back before we get soaked?"

"I want more of this."

"The no-see-ums or rain?"

"All of it. I want to live, not simply chase one goal after another that leaves me empty. If I told you that I lived more in the realm of the dead than I ever have in the land of the living, would you believe me?"

"Son, anything you ever tell me about where you go in your head when you experience an absence seizure, I'd believe. But you know your mother's not going to want you to be gone now that her tumor is shrinking. If she recovers from this like the doctors think she will, maybe we'll simply buy a boat."

"A ship," I replied. "A big one like a windjammer that's fore-and-aft rigged. You know how to run things, supervise a crew. Mom is great at getting people to do things and work as a team." I gestured toward the oncoming storm and the anchorage where our rented sailboat floated. "This is not all there is, not even close to all, and I don't want to waste a moment filling in bubbles on an exam just so I can get into college and fill in more bubbles. There are treasures out there we can't even imagine, and I plan on finding them."

"I'm sure you will, Son. I'm certain if anyone can, you will."